Omar McCann

thank you so

much for allowing me to share

this story with you.

Hope you enjoy it.

thanks again

Jur Anderson ☺

01/29/07

JACK McCAMEY
2166 3 Rd. St.
Trenton, MI 48183-2100

...on the Doorsteps of Heaven

by

James J. Giordano

Bloomington, IN Milton Keynes, UK

authorHOUSE®

AuthorHouse™
1663 Liberty Drive, Suite 200
Bloomington, IN 47403
www.authorhouse.com
Phone: 1-800-839-8640

AuthorHouse™ UK Ltd.
500 Avebury Boulevard
Central Milton Keynes, MK9 2BE
www.authorhouse.co.uk
Phone: 08001974150

First published by AuthorHouse 12/18/2006

ISBN: 978-1-4259-8287-4 (sc)

Printed in the United States of America
Bloomington, Indiana

This book is printed on acid-free paper.

My Book Dedication:

Mary Jane…you are my inspiration
To my sons, Christopher and Andrew… you are my life
Thank you Mom and Dad for loving me
To all of my family whom I love dearly
To all of my friends that I have ever known…my
significant others
and to….
Compassion, Forgiveness and Love…without you I
could not exist…

Table of Contents

Day	1
Moms and Dads	12
Howdy Neighbor!	15
Magnetic Attraction	19
"Weather" You Like it or Not	23
Drive Time	26
Dis and Dat	32
Ice Time	42
The Gardner	54
…on the Doorsteps of Heaven	60
Significance	71
Family Ties	90
Exploring	95
Harry and Bottle	111
"Husband…Father, killed in Spectacular Crash"	120
A Puzzling Situation	123
Parachute	129
Lost and Found	137
The End	138
Epilogue…Love Letters	139

Day

"Joy in looking and comprehending is nature's most beautiful gift."---Albert Einstein

I found myself tossing and turning the night away, 3am and still no sleep! If only there was a method to disconnect the neurons within the sanctuary of my brain, just for awhile so I might be able to drift off with my dreams. Unfortunately this was another night as many before and surely thousands of times after, where I lay awake in bed to the multitude of images and thoughts piercing my grey matter. If you don't know where the switch is, you simply cannot turn it off.

Similar to most people, the day to day struggles and challenges in life often times keep me thinking and pondering, trying to make sense of it all and always searching to simply understand and maybe even solve the problems of mine, my families' and sometimes even the difficulties in the world itself. What a night, what a day!

There was though an almost spiritual quiet and calm that surrounded me in my home… dark and silent, and instead of wasting my time and efforts in my struggle for sleep, I got up and felt for my warm and soft slippers that immediately caressed my icy toes. It was the middle of January and even with the furnace running, the cold on the hardwood floor sent a chill thru my 50-year old body. As tired as I was, I dragged my feet and headed downstairs in search of the morning newspaper.

The hours from about 2am to 5am are quite remarkable because it is a time when I find myself thinking at a level of clarity that is almost perfect. In bed, I am a cluster of thoughts bashing up against each other with no discernable pattern, no rhyme and no reason, but once I am up, and if it is that special time of the morning, the almost complete silence and darkness surrounding me, sparks my thoughts to become more focused.

Shuffling my feet down the narrow stairs to the front door entrance, I searched for my morning newspaper. Rarely was it on the front porch, but more often it would be found on the sidewalk, in the shrubs or on the lawn. There it was, about 20 yards in the distance, lying on the middle of the driveway. Clearly the effort to retrieve the paper on this morning was going to be a struggle. How on earth explorers are able to trudge and plow thru the fierce weather of Antarctica or the Himalayas is truly remarkable and a feat to be respected and admired. Now here I was walking thru maybe a half foot of snow and ice at 3:15am with a wind chill below zero and my struggle was monumental! Obviously an *Ernest H.Shackelton* I am not.

With coffee in hand and the newspaper in front of me, I sat back in my chair, relaxed and comforted. The silence of the night did me good, and my fatigue had all but vanished. Immediately I pulled out the sports section to catch the latest happenings and scores of my favorite teams. With speed, skill, physical and mental toughness, ice hockey has all the elements of pure excitement and drama. It is the sport I enjoy the most and on this early morning I could see that my favorite team, the *Detroit Red Wings,* was doing quite well, even though several key players were out with injuries. Where would the *Wings* be without *Yzerman, Shanny, Lidstrom, Chelios,* and *McCarty?* In Detroit, or *Hockeytown* as we call it, the *Wings* are almost like a religion. The thrills of wins and *Stanley Cup* championships are always a buzz around this city; a city that often times yearns for respect.

Newspaper clippings: **Boston archdiocese to relent, sell residence...Proceeds to help pay clergy abuse victims...Ohio shootings put parents on edge...Man's death ruled homicide in fight with cops...London: Man charged in bomb conspiracy...Jerusalem: Possible**

attack stopped... a full page ad that read... ***What the new prescription drug benefit will do for you...no sound bites, no spin, no politics. Just the facts.***

Indeed, this is an interesting and dynamic world represented by all types of people with different ideas and diverse agendas... all clamoring to catch my attention on this blustery morning. The prescription ad was if anything...amusing, particularly because as honest as it tried to come across, it was at least to this reader, a disingenuous blurb of babble. Let's be candid; when they say *no spin*, you know that is exactly what it is. When they profess *no politics*, then you know it has everything to do with politics, and when it reads *just the facts*, you can be sure they are the facts as they (the advertiser) see it. If you have to preempt your ad with these declarations, then chances are you're not being totally honest. The truth needs no defense or disclaimers.

In the silence of the morning, I read the obvious articles and stories that newspapers need to tell in order to sell their product...murder, disasters, health issues that on a daily basis contradict themselves. You know; one day a vitamin or food product is healthy for you and then a day, month or year later that same item is found to cause cancer or increase your cholesterol or interact with your prescription medication. People love reading about life on the edge, the morbid, the horrific, and the outlandish. We feed on the misfortunes, tragedies and struggles of others as if they were a necessary part of our diet. Although I am not a psychologist, I would have to say, this mode of behavior is rather commonplace. Maybe a way to distract ourselves from our own trials and tribulations is to seek pleasure in the pain of others, after all who doesn't enjoy a juicy story of some celebrity in a barrel full of hot water. At times I have found myself in the glee of it all, only to eventually corral my feelings and come to the realization that this simply cannot be a *good thing.*

About 4am I could hear a scampering, thumping sound on the roof of the house. In the quiet and solace of the morning, the noises were a bit startling but not frightening, and in a fraction of a second it was obvious the clatter came from a squirrel or two playing around or searching for something to eat. I suppose squirrels sleep, but not on this frigid morning. Finally I caught a glimpse of my fat furry brown friends dashing across the front snow covered lawn, only to take a flying leap onto a large maple tree near the edge of the icy street. Really, it was like a ballet or maybe like an *Olympic* gymnast, because the graceful technique these particular squirrels displayed, as they ran and soared so effortlessly, was an astounding sight to witness. Though I had seen their athleticism time and time again, on this remarkable morning, I just marveled in awe at how wonderful these creatures truly were.

I pondered…did they agonize about their lives or have any clue how precarious their existence was, living in hostile weather, or being among humans who regularly (and often times without concern) ran over their fellow squirrels with automobiles? Maybe to never fully grasp or comprehend one's fate; the realization of life and death is a blessing. Human beings have a more sophisticated innate sense of self, and our understanding of life and death is our fortune but it is also our torment.

My unfinished cup of coffee felt cool in my hands and while my slippers are my feet warmers, so is my coffee cup for my hands. A quick zap in the microwave oven and once again I could see the steam curling upward and giving off the wonderful rich aroma of *Folgers*. My hands caressed the silver and black ceramic cup and the warmth immediately relieved my fingers of the morning cold. It was so quiet in my home and I delighted in every second of it!

Religion is an important and always relevant issue concerning humanity because it has the ability and formidable power to dictate the very way people live, and the effects of religious beliefs are felt everyday in our society. As I continued to scan the newspaper it was evident that numerous skirmishes and wars fought in the world are more often based on opposing religious beliefs, and the sad undeniable reality is, is that our lack of understanding pertaining to other religions creates opposition and this ignorance breeds envy, distrust and hatred. Even in our own country where hundreds, perhaps thousands of religions are practiced, the animosity is evident. We are so confident that our faith is the chosen one, and because of this folly, our patience and understanding of other religions is tenuous. We boast, brag and even flaunt our beliefs as if we have the only key to *Heaven* itself, yet deep inside many of us conceal our skepticism. I admit, I do have my own doubts.

A *Robert M.Pirsig* once said, "You are never dedicated to something you have complete confidence in. Nobody is fanatically shouting that the sun is going to rise tomorrow. They know it is going to rise tomorrow. When people are fanatically dedicated to political or religious faiths or any other kind of dogmas or goals, it's because these dogmas or goals are in doubt."

The bottom line is we have to keep convincing ourselves what we believe in is legitimate and true, and the best way to achieve this goal is to be stiff in our resolve with little or no compromise.

I was brought up in the *Roman Catholic* religion by two very wonderful parents, and with my three brothers and sister, we were taught how to practice our faith according to the teachings of *Jesus Christ*. As a child, I was schooled in the belief that my religion as a Catholic was the one true belief and other faiths were flawed. Indeed, this is practically true with any religion, where it is imperative that what is taught is the only truth. So is it any surprise why there is so much religious tension and strife on this planet?

As time went on and I became an adult, my skepticism grew concerning my faith, and while I still had many questions, most of them remained unsolved. Often, I would find myself in the middle of the night praying to *God*, and asking him to appear and talk with me, and grant me the answers I was seeking. My pleas went unanswered and soon my faith remained a distant remnant of the past. My background in the sciences and math in college became my truths and as time passed, I would use this knowledge to assist and help me to understand how circumstances in this universe of ours worked minus a *God*. It's funny, maybe ironic, but in some ways it is more difficult not to believe in *God*. With *God*, you can explain off many mysteries of the world by simply saying that "only *God* knows", or "*God* has his reasons", or "*God's* ways are not our ways."

Faith is a key word concerning religion, because with faith you don't need to explain the many contradictions or mysterious events that occur all around us. All one needs to do is *believe.* For me, it was a lonely feeling being aware that so many people I knew, held on to their beliefs with no questions, while I could not even remotely interpret the meaning of my life with *God.* It is a grim and desolate feeling to believe that when you die, that, that is it...never again to be with your spouse, children, parents, siblings, friends...never to enjoy a crisp autumn afternoon or even the simple pleasure of a banana split. On average, we only live (if we are fortunate) for 70 to 90 years, and anybody my age or older knows exactly how lightning fast time goes by. Is this all there is?

Like all living things, human beings instinctively want to live and will do everything possible to keep it that way. Without those instincts we would become extinct as a species or at best our chances for survival would become greatly diminished. Could this instinct be one of the more obvious reasons for the creation of religion and *God?* After all, if we don't want to die into "*nothing-ness*", then why not create a *God* and *Heaven* so when our physical body dies, our spirit or soul will transcend to a better place, a utopia, a *Heaven?* Does believing in a *God* give us a purpose? Does religion, which causes so much chaos, also create order in the world, where we are given rules and values to follow and thereby keeping the masses in a controlled and well-behaved moralistic mode of living? I know there are many others that have similar feelings about religion, but I understand how difficult it is to just come out and say it. It is certainly not *politically correct* to doubt the existence of *God*, even though many that espouse *God's* existence (i.e. televangelism) are the very ones who denigrate it. Religion is too often used as a political tool or a money-making enterprise in this country and around the world, and the real meaning behind those religions becomes a maze of mush... indistinguishable and maligned. I find that repugnant.

Peering thru the frosted window, the faint glimmer of sunlight was starting to make its grand entrance for the new day. In the foreground, the scantily clad trees appeared almost skeleton-like and wisps of clouds were dancing with the rhythm of the blowing wind. So inspiring, yet such a somber look at this moment in time when my part of the world was just rising from their slumber. My coffee cooled down, and as I placed the cup onto the fine but cluttered oak table, I realized as I have before, moments in time like this I am indebted to for just having a life.

There are so many wonders all around us, yet many of us choose to ignore the beauty, the absolutely astounding pleasures this planet has to offer us. One hundred years from this very second, most living things alive today will not even be in existence, which to me suggests that we as human beings have a very short time to absorb the richness and glory of life. If for the moment we concede there is no life after death, then would it not make even more sense to breathe in the fullness of our existence and let it capture our hearts and minds to the *enth* degree?

Like lemmings to the cliffs, we run without a reason or purpose, and we race by people and events that are ever so meaningful to us, as we jump to our fate into the abyss. Time is so short in our fast and furious lives and to squander even a moment of it is our loss, a loss that cannot be recovered.

There was a warm and restful sense of comfort within myself on this frozen wintry daybreak, my thoughts complete...on the last day of my life.

"Minutes are worth more than money. Spend them wisely."
---Thomas P. Murphy

Moms and Dads

"Good parents give their children roots and wings. Roots to know where home is, wings to fly away and exercise what's been taught them."---Jonas Salk

Scanning thru the living room window, the sun's rays found their way to my closed eyes calling me to wake up to the new day. The distant sound of the radio alarm could be heard with the infectious laughter of *Drew and Mike, WRIF* radio. Apparently in the very early hours of the morning, I settled down on the comfortable royal blue couch with a tan cotton throw blanket over myself. It was a sparkling clear Monday morning, with typical winter temperatures in the single digits and a stiff breeze out of the west. Peering into the neighborhood, I could see sparkling icicles in the thousands tightly clinging to the roof overhangs of the homes and large clumps of snow and ice weighing down the sturdy branches of the trees and evergreens. Though harsh at times, Michigan winter weather and the beauty it brings is a marvel to witness.

Funny how time plays tricks with our memories, for it was only but a few hours ago I was quietly meditating and sipping my coffee in the early morning, yet the event already seemed as if it never occurred or at best was long ago. When you think about it, what happened to you even a second ago is no closer to you than what happened 5 years in the past. Neither event will ever occur again, so the distances they leave behind are exactly the same.

"Come on Andrew! It's getting late...let's not be tardy for class!"

Being a parent is not only the most challenging responsibility, but also undoubtedly one of the most difficult. From a practical point of view, raising children is always a first time experience because each child is different...unique, and while you must rely on life empiricism as a guide, sometimes even the best plans can go amiss. My love and life MJ and I have been parents for 23 years, raising two remarkable but very different boys, Christopher 23 and Andrew 17. Wonderful they are, but neither one had been a cake walk when it came to parenting, and inevitably it was often the case (and not necessarily a *good thing*) that our *methods* of handling problems were not always on the same page. You really do need a *plan*, a coordinated plan when it comes to Mom and Dad being on the same team. If I call a pass play down the sidelines and Mom tries to take a handoff, well either you are going to lose yards or you might get *lucky* and somehow manage to have a positive gain. *Lucky* seldom occurs. Usually you end up with a busted play and there you are, back to square one. Children are intelligent human beings (more than we give them credit for), and they sense the disharmony, and ultimately will capitalize on the situation.

Never will I admit to being an indefectible parent, because I continue to make parental miscues routinely, and it has taken me years to realize that it does not make me a bad person or parent, and it certainly is not indicative of the quality persons my two sons have become. As a parent, I have come to grasp that it is essential to roll with the punches or be knocked out. Don't torture yourself or bang your "*noggin*" up against the wall by trying to be the quintessential parent, but rather use your energies to be with your children as often as you can and simply *love* them.

On this crisp wintry morning, I was about to discover what I had been pursuing my entire life. It was not what I expected.

Howdy Neighbor!

"You can't depend on your eyes when your imagination is out of focus."---Mark Twain

Superstition has never been an integral component concerning the way I perceive the world...*knock on wood.* I believe that circumstances happen due to a domino effect, where event upon event eventually leads to an occurrence or outcome, good, bad or indifferent. To presuppose that an outcome of such an event is due to some force beyond humanity and that there is some cryptic or spiritual implication to it all (whatever *it* may be), is in my humble opinion without true merit. There is though a preponderance of people on this planet that live their lives with a powerful belief in *spirits* (if you will) among us changing and creating events. It is after all instinctive to want and desire explanations about the unexplainable. Let me digress.

Human beings need discovery...exploration, and frankly we aren't patient waiting for the answers. There simply are no quick fixes...ask any scientist or explorer. History, however, does show that humanity has been on a searching expedition for a very long time, and this is a *good thing*, after all, it is the insatiable craving for knowledge that has led mankind to major scientific discoveries of our universe.

Now back to the ghosts. Spiritual discovery is entirely another matter and usually requires little or no proof to back it up. This would appear at least on the surface...a *quick fix*. Admittedly, when it comes to religion, spirits, and the belief in God, I often times use a considerable amount of my energies trying to discredit circumstances or beliefs that cannot be explained or proved, and where *faith* is the only answer to the question. But, you know what? I will confess that I could be wrong...wrong when it comes to religion and the belief in God. I honestly just don't know, and the questions and mysteries never stop coming. You would think, the older you get, the questions should be less and the answers easier to figure out, but the reality is the exact opposite.

Here are a few thoughts; did you ever think about your own demise... when will it occur and in what manner? Do we simply choose to ignore and pretend that our lives will go on forever? Are we afraid to ponder the inevitable or are we just impervious? Questions...questions.

The deep blue winter sky was alive with the artistry of the wind blowing and pushing, using the clouds to create lines and shapes into a collage of whimsical images. As the artist painted the pictures across the infinite sky, it also howled and whistled a morning melody familiar to me. Against my face, the cold slapped me over and over again, causing my eyes to water and nose to run. Ah yes, the "*running nose*"…sounds like an interesting *Nike* commercial. Immediately I sought the welcoming shelter of my car. It had been running for about 15 minutes so that it would be warm for my jaunt to Andrew's school and then off to work.

The extreme contrast of the frigid cold to the calming warmth of the inner sanctum of my automobile was a superb pleasure. I could almost visualize the warm air gently massaging the exposed parts of myself, relieving me of the discomforting algidity. Now if it was simply a warm day and I entered the car, I never would have had that very satisfying sensation to my body.

You would think, the average person doesn't consciously think of these spontaneous and maybe idle thoughts, (maybe I am a bit persnickety at times), but I suspect that most members of humanity have very active imaginations. The problem is, is that we often times repress these capricious thoughts even though it is for our own pleasure. It can be fun......I do seriously think so.

Speaking of imagination, I have always imagined that people generally want to be liked (duh! You think so?) and to reinforce that notion; I occasionally played a game with my boys and their friends when we would drive thru the neighborhood. The game was called "*howdy neighbor!*" What we would do is have the car windows down, spot a stranger who was cutting his lawn or maybe just sitting on his porch, and then we would wave energetically and scream out, "**howdy neighbor!**" Almost always, that stranger would look up; smile and wave back to us. My suspicions that people generally yearn to be warm, courteous and friendly to each other were proven, at least to me, by this harmless, simple and fun game.

Andrew at his usual *fast pace* finally found his way to the car and off to school we went. Our morning conversation was typical on this day...silence followed by more silence. While the early morning was a sure fire tonic for me, it was almost *sedative-like* for him, and while we both cared for and loved each other, it was an unwritten rule that it was best for me to harness my energy and allow Andrew to slowly *warm up*. Arriving at school, Andrew opened the car door, quietly said "good-bye", and headed out to his classes. I always would say "see ya...I love you...have a great day," but I am afraid it was so routine, it almost assuredly got lost in the shuffle.

Another moment in time, I thought to myself, a moment already sucked into the mysterious black hole of the past...never to return.

Magnetic Attraction

"Fear not that your life will someday end; fear only that you do nothing about it."---Unknown

Diego was a very trustworthy and dependable truck driver for an automobile parts company located on the outskirts of Mexico City, Mexico. Although he was only in his early 30's, his rough facial features were desert-like, dry, cracked and pitted. Diego had been a hard working fellow since he was just a small child, and he would usually do whatever it took to make a wage for his elderly parents and his own family that included his wife Maria and two young boys. For Diego, life was difficult, but his Catholic faith kept him going, always attending mass on Sunday and regularly praying to the Virgin Mary for strength and guidance.

It was a January morning when he received an urgent call from his company. Due to unforeseen circumstances, they were short drivers, and even though Diego had just finished a long and arduous cross country drive from Mexico City to Trenton, New Jersey, he was needed again on this short notice to make a run to Michigan in order to deliver a specific auto part that was a replacement for a component that had been recalled. This part had something to do with the wheel bearings on certain automobiles. Apparently the defective part in some of the vehicles would snap on a sudden stop and turn of the wheel, rendering the automobile to lose control. Exhausted as he was, Diego always needed the money and he knew how fortunate it was just to be employed. So without hesitation, Diego packed up his gear and gave his wife a loving embrace and kissed his two sons goodbye.

It just so happened, on my refrigerator, I recently had placed a magnet onto an official- looking piece of mail I received concerning a recall on my vehicle…something about wheel bearings…I think. On top of the notice, I positioned a thank-you note over it and then held it onto the refrigerator with the same magnet. This particular magnet was the *Detroit Red Wing* official schedule and it was large and strong enough to hold both letters without falling.

Have you ever seen how people decorate and clutter…I mean cover their refrigerators? If I were in the business of selling refrigerators, I believe I would have them adorned with all sorts of magnets. Maybe it would be a good selling point. Know what I mean?

"Yes mam, don't be concerned about how much food you can stuff in this puppy, but just look with delight at all of the magnets you can use. Our company estimates that our Magnet-o-rator refrigerator can hold up to 500 various sized magnets and that is just for the door! For an extra $250 we can give you an additional 5 year limited warranty that will guarantee your magnets will never fall off, and if they do, we will send someone (a magnetechanic) right over to your home and fix the problem!"

The old saying, *out of sight, out of mind*, certainly held true concerning my official recall letter. The thank-you note covering the recall notice was without doubt a wonderful thing and all I really wanted, was for my family to see that my profession as a Pharmacist truly had its rewards.

Mr.I called me one day at the pharmacy and said that Mrs.I was suffering from mild to severe headaches. He assumed she was having a migraine or cluster headache as she had in the past, and because the symptoms of blurred vision and nausea were present. Pharmacists know how common this is in our line of work; you get a call and are asked an assortment of questions concerning medications, and/or medical conditions. I have never pretended to be a Physician, and over the years I have always respected their unique abilities, but Pharmacists often times are at the front lines when a Doctor is not available, usually in the capacity to offer professional advice, especially when it concerns over-the-counter or prescription medications. In this aspect, Pharmacists are uniquely qualified…and frankly, the most accessible health professional (in my opinion) is the neighborhood Pharmacist. Knowing that Mrs.I was not a young woman and had a history of heart disease, hypertension and diabetes, I advised Mr.I to take her immediately to the hospital emergency room. As it turned out, she was having mini-strokes and going to the hospital probably prevented her from having a major stroke. Several months later, Mr.I and Mrs.I sent me a cheerful note thanking me for my part in their ordeal. It was a gratifying feeling to know that I helped out, and well…I just had to put that letter on the refrigerator… *front and center*…even if it meant covering up some other message.

Remember when I said, "Circumstances happen due to a domino effect, where event upon event eventually leads to an occurrence or outcome, good, bad or indifferent"? The *dominos* for Diego and I were stacked; and without warning they began to tumble. Quite unexpectedly, my life was about to change…a search finally would end and a new journey would begin.

"Weather" You Like it or Not

"Ancient Egyptians believed that upon death they would be asked two questions, and their answers would determine whether they would continue their journey to the afterlife. The first question was, "Did you bring joy?" The second was, "Did you find joy?"
---Leo Buscaglia

Life altering changes can occur at any moment, but typically we fail to consider these occurrences until they actually happen. Yes, we do buy smoke alarms, life insurance, medical insurance and insurance for insurance to secure the possessions we have and to protect the lives and security of our loved ones. Somehow, and too often, we do see ourselves as impenetrable to life's calamities and move on. The most significant life altering change is death, and this grim happening leaves us little or no time to think.

Imagine yourself enjoying a wonderful lifestyle, residing in the sunshine state of Florida. You just received a promotion for all your hard and dedicated work and with that accomplishment; a generous bonus is also given to you. When you arrive home, you tell your spouse and children the great news. Life is grand! The insects outside are buzzing and chirping as they always do on this muggy August evening and all is right with your universe. You retire for the evening in the comfort of your charming home you have worked so enthusiastically for, and then drift off to sleep with your dreams.

For several days there had been a widespread low-pressure drop in your peaceful town, and the *National Weather Service* issued a warning of severe thunderstorms and a possible risk of tornados. With today's miraculous technology, weather forecasting can be a very accurate science. Weather predicting, though, can never be 100% and of course is subject to error. You have heard the warnings before and tonight you just kind of ignored it, especially because when you went to bed, the weather was calm, peaceful and soothing…nothing to worry about.

The super cell forming off the Gulf coast had been brewing and once it hit land, the violent rotating vortex of an F-5 tornado slammed hard, without much warning and with no mercy or compassion.

All you ever were is no more, whatever problems or difficulties you had…gone, and yes, you never really had time to consider this definite life altering change. This of course is but a tiny speck of the innumerable methods that belong to the grim reaper's repertoire. He swoops down on you...no jury, no negotiations...no chance.

As far as lives go, my life to this point was rather typical and ordinary. Being married, raising a family and pursuing my career relatively consumed the way I carried on with my life. Believe me, this was *not* a *bad thing*, but I had always suspected there had to be more to the puzzle of my life and the missing pieces were still out there for me to find. Maybe those pieces were there but out of my grasp, or maybe I just couldn't fathom or understand the magnitude or gravity of it all when it came to the importance of one small...seemingly *insignificant* life... mine.

Life is full of extraordinary questions that do not necessarily have extraordinary answers or explanations. I was about to find this out.

> *"Dying seems less sad than have lived too little."*
> *---Gloria Steinem*

Drive Time

"Don't sacrifice your life to work and ideals. The most important things in life are human relations. I found that out too late."
---Katharinde Susannah Prichard, Australian author

The frenzy of prime time morning rush hour was in full swing and I was one of the willing participants. This most definitely was a chapter taken out of Darwin's *Origin of the Species*, because this morning's drive time was the survival of the fittest. Like the Serengeti Plains of Africa, the automobiles, trucks, vans, suvs, and rigs were figuratively transformed into wildebeests, zebras, and Thompson's gazelles, all…by the way, in a mad migratory dash for the proverbial life-saving water hole. Survival was the number one priority and to observe this instinctive behavior at the point of attack was a vision to behold. Surrounding us were lions, wild dogs, cheetahs and hyenas…ever watchful, lurking and stalking to take full advantage of any slight weakness that might be exposed.

I could see the heavy breathing as the frigid temperatures created clouds of air exiting the exhaust pipes, and the light snow across the icy pavement would swirl and twirl an exotic dance as the grabbing and gripping ebony paws seized the earth at flashing speeds. Experience on this hazardous trek was the best possible weapon for survival, because if you had not been down this particular trail before, you would surly become prey to the predators. In the distance, maybe a quarter mile ahead of me I spotted a sleek *Lexus* suv with a spectacular metallic gray mane and jet-black paws that ripped and grooved the highway with lightning acceleration. As he raced thru the underpass, he was instantly pounced upon by an even more impressive metal beast with a piercing siren and flashing lights of silver, blue and red that literally stunned the arrogant *Lexus* creature into submission. It was a jungle out there!

A furious winter wind was blowing out of the west and repeatedly jolted and jostled the small automobile I was driving. It was a dependable car, and I enjoyed the 40 minute drive to work. My experience of traversing across this asphalt plain allowed me confidence, and it gave me pause on this morning to analyze my thoughts.

The phrase, "life isn't fair" is a cliché, probably used too frequently (oxymoron alert!), but is commonly spoken because life constantly is throwing us curve balls that often times make us flail away and miss. It is a cry for help, a feeling of impotence, and a constant reminder, cautioning us that from the beginning to the end of our lives, things rarely will be easy. We use terms like "*go with the flow*", or "*oh well, what can you do?*" as our surrender statements elucidating instances or circumstances in our lives that we feel are not in our control. Although I have capitulated to many of life's potholes, it does not mean for one moment that I have been enamored by them. There are numerous things I have always considered *unfair*, and on this morning's *drive time*, I thought of a few.

Monopolies; are there not anti-trust laws in this country that are supposed to prevent this? Would it really surprise anyone to eventually see a world controlled by just a handful of corporations (we're almost there) that will manipulate the populous and pull the strings of the government to do their biddings? In fact, is the government the biggest monopoly of all? Think about it! How many laws are created with the real approval or vote of the common man? Do citizens get to vote yes or no on the various tax increases that have stifled their earnings and decreased their quality of life? Why do senators and representatives see themselves as *celebrities* and not lawmakers for the people? Although these elected government officials are supposed to be civil servants to their constituents, the reality of it all, is the common citizen *serves them*! Today representatives, represent themselves and the large corporations that support them. Certainly the term *corprasentatives* is a more appropriate word to describe these parasites that infest this land we call home. Let's be truthful; numerous elected government officials in this country like to stay cozy with corporate America because that is where the financial support and power comes from. Together a formidable team is conceived and the average Joe doesn't have a chance. They make the rules and you obey.

In the United States, we proudly display to the world our home-grown corporations and we let everyone know how we are the economic machine of the planet, yet companies we look to as *American* can be deceiving. Today these corporations are international conglomerates with little allegiance to anyone. Patriotism within these giants is only something displayed when it is for show or when there is some advantage to be gained by them. Is anyone even remotely surprised that countries like Mexico, India and especially China are taking away millions of jobs from Americans and there is absolutely nothing of any real substance being done about it? These *American* companies race to other countries, leaving millions of U.S. workers in the dust, abandoning them to be forgotten and discarding them as you would any piece of trash. Do you think for one moment that your basic human rights are not being stripped away slowly but surly? The once solid foundation that was the strength of this country is showing serious signs of fatigue…it is starting to crumble. When a country loses compassion and deserts its citizens, and when there is that "*everyone for themselves*" mentality, hope is lost and the love and trust of our fellow man is strained.

The highway in a relatively short period of time was transformed into an ice rink. I could view the shine and glimmer coming off the pavement and my vehicle awkwardly skimmed across the mirror-like road, much like a first time ice skater would. The slightly balding tires on my automobile desperately tried to hug the road but with little success and my inattention to my precarious surroundings for just a split-second caused me to misjudge my handling of the situation. In front of me at about a hundred yards or so an 18-wheeler had jack-knifed and the cab along with the trailer had flipped over on its side. It was like a bulls-eye for me. Hitting my brakes and turning my wheel at an irresponsible 55 miles an hour was of course a colossal error. It seems to me as I recall, a cracking or snapping sound in the vicinity of the front drivers-side wheel, but it was an incidental thought compared to the magnitude of smashing into this huge carcass of a rig. At that instant, I could see my vehicle crumpling and grinding in on me…an air bag deployment, and then quickly followed by screaming and wailing pieces of sharp metal, piercing my chest and neck.

My feelings of curiosity and astonishment overwhelmed any fear or terror that I assumed I might experience, especially considering the gory mess in front of me. Was this real? I gazed out of the busted windshield viewing the overturned cab and for the first time, I encountered Diego. Without really knowing the exact physics of what happens when a vehicle collides into a much larger object than itself (how about ka-boom!) and how everything plays out, I could not explain how Diego's body was found lying stomach down on the mashed up hood of my car with his face staring ever so peacefully at me. A quiet, almost soothing appearance bathed his rugged face; eyes open with a *Mona Lisa* grin. Like Niagara Falls, the red was gushing and pouring out of my body, and I...well, I introduced myself to Diego.

"*Howdy neighbor!*" I feebly said to him with maybe the most sincere smile that I ever had.

Like a spider furiously wrapping its prey, a tremendous whoosh of cold seemed to spin and circle my mangled body. At that moment, I knew all too well, there were going to be no second chances. Death was paying me a visit and he didn't even have the common courtesy to let me know he was coming.

My thoughts were of my family, my eyes as Diego's remained open, and my existence on earth had ended. It was time to move on.

Dis and Dat

"Remember this, very little is needed to make a happy life."
---Marcus Aurelius Antonius

A delicate breeze fueled by pleasantly warm temperatures this summer afternoon meandered thru the golden meadow. It gently massaged and pushed against the tall grass, creating a rhythmic kind of dance choreographed to perfection, and as it passed upon the colorful array of blooming flowers, it would playfully scoop up the pleasing aromatic scents they offered and then disperse the fragrances into the open air for all to enjoy. The centerpiece of this tranquil meadow was a sparkling pond, oblong in shape, partially surrounded by tall reeds and inhabited by a wide variety of animals and insects. This small body of water was being fed by an underground spring, and even though the pond seemed still and silent, the natural pump below kept the water moving and purified. On this particular summer day, the heat from the life-giving sun kept the pond at a comfortable temperature, making it enjoyable for the creatures, such as the birds, frogs and turtles. The fish below seemed oblivious to minor details like water temperature and turned their main attention to the smorgasbord of insects that frequented the surface of the pond. Although it was the official landing-strip for the mosquitoes, horseflies, dragonflies, and hundreds of other insect species, it was done at great risk, as multiple schools of fish keenly eyed and monitored the surface for the slightest disruption of water. This little ecosystem was alive and well…in perfect harmony and motion.

Dis and Dat were having the time of their lives on this sun-filled day. Both were mature bullfrogs in their prime, and this wonderful pond they lived in was their playground and home. The two frogs were friends from the moment they encountered each other as tiny tadpoles. At first, they would feed together by filtering bits of algae from the water and eventually as they transformed into frogs, they became very adept at snatching unsuspecting insects. They were fortunate…Dis and Dat, because the life of a tadpole or frog is dangerous. Many of their friends would fall victim to the multitude of predators around them, like fish, snakes, salamanders and birds, but somehow the two friends were able to remain relatively anonymous and grow into maturity.

The two best friends were quite different in physical appearance and personality, and if opposites do attract, then this possibly was the best explanation as to why Dis and Dat were always at each other's sides. Dis was all he could be, at the top of the heap for bull frogs. He measured almost 20 cm in length, with sparkling smooth skin and large webbed feet. His telltale yellow throat, large eardrums and immense size gave him an intimidating appearance to the other frogs of the pond. His large eyes and nostrils situated at the top of his head were always in perfect sync as he stealthily and cautiously remained just above the surface of the water where he was excellently camouflaged by matching the bottom of the pond. With his razor sharp vision and lightning-like speed, he could easily spot a dragonfly slightly grazing the watery plain and in an instant, snap it into his large gaping mouth. Nobody did it better than Dis. Although they both were born around the same time, Dat was considerably smaller than his "*buddy*", and probably because Dis was always at his side, Dat was able to defy his evolutionary fate in the universe.

Dis had an imposing personality that demanded others to respect him…after all; he was the *king* of the pond. A serious thinker to a fault, Dis never seemed satisfied…a discontented *frog-fellow* you might say. Too frequently he would evaluate his life as simply dismal and ordinary and to him there had to be more than the pond and the repetitive existence he was living in. Although he enjoyed his friends, his best friend Dat, and his lofty high ranking among them, it just never seemed enough for him and this quite naturally made Dis, not always the easiest bullfrog to be around with. Dat on the other hand was easy going, playful and just giddy-go-happy to be in the beautiful surroundings of the pond in the meadow. The commonality between the two friends was a fierce loyalty developed over the years and there truly wasn't anything that either of them wouldn't do for the other…even if it meant risking or giving one's life.

As a matter of fact, it had been just a few days ago when Dis and Dat were playing their own version of leapfrog, jumping great distances from one rock to another. It was terrific exercise and Dis thought it would help Dat develop stronger legs so that he could evade predators more easily. A frog is a frog after all, and that being said, a frog really has very limited tools at his disposal to protect himself with. Instinct, camouflage, quickness and the ability to have expert leaping abilities is a key to a frog's survival. By having these abilities perfected, an attack could hopefully be evaded by quickly jumping into the pond and diving to safety below the surface.

High above, in the deep blue sky, a circling hawk was keenly watching the movements of the pond below. Its large and highly developed eyes could very easily spot the smallest of creatures even though it was soaring at such a high altitude. The frogs in the pond were always on the look-out because they knew all too well that hawks were without a doubt…deadly. This flying enemy above was a constant danger and was extremely capable of swooping down, at a moments notice, with blazing speed and stealth, grab its prey with sharp long talons and then at leisure rip its prize apart with its strong hooked bill. As cruel and horrible as a hawk would seem, it is just acting out its own natural behavior in order for it to survive; no different than Dis swallowing down an unsuspecting dragonfly.

In an instant of experience and good fortune, Dis caught a glimpse of the kamikaze-like dive of the determined hawk heading straight toward Dat. Dis made a desperate but very accurately timed leap toward the oblivious Dat and just as the hawk's talons were ready to grab hold of him, Dis's large and lunging body hit the back side of the hawk's legs causing the predator's timing to be off for the miss. Dis's body still pulsating forward struck Dat and into the water they went. Needless to say, they hurried to safety at the bottom of the pond. Over the years, Dis made similar heroic efforts when it came to protecting his friends and his best pal Dat.

On this day though, the pond was relatively calm, and Dis and Dat were resting comfortably on a large boulder protruding above the water surface, observing the human children who were playing on the waters edge under the ever watchful eyes of their parents. About a quarter mile away from the pond was a small town, and it was the citizens of this tiny municipality that constructed a few benches along the shore. Here they could sit and relax, watch their children, enjoy the solitude and witness the sheer beauty of the area.

"Oh how I long to be one of those humans," sighed Dis.

"I know you always say that, but I really could never understand why?" questioned Dat. "What do you really know about them except that they are much larger than we are? We don't even understand their language and for all you know, they may not be happy creatures like we are. In fact, I would guess at best, they have as many problems as we do. Dis...my dearest friend... *you* and *I* are frogs. Know what? That is a *good thing* and it is enough for me. Your intense interest in these unknown beings has become your obsession and it has made you unhappy and longing. I can only tell you, your friends and I will always be here for you and we respect you because we know who you are. Do you know who you are?"

Alas, Dis would have nothing of it because his admiration for these mysterious beings went to the point of adoration and worship. Dis knew his friend a considerate thinker, and he learned to take his wisdom to heart. The issue though with the humans was a hurdle he just couldn't overcome and so it was that very evening, Dis secretly went to the north side of the pond where he heard of a magical and mystical turtle named Amee. Dis was seeking answers regarding his desire to become human, and the reputation of this wise and ancient turtle brought Dis to the mud hole where Amee resided.

Indeed, Amee was an enigma to the animals of the pond. She mostly kept to herself, but when called upon, legends and stories say that her wisdom went beyond time and her unearthly powers were beyond understanding and explanation. Now, for the first time, Dis laid his eyes upon the wondrous Amee. Frankly, she seemed quite ordinary, he thought. Her carapace, or upper shell, was smooth and it had a color of dark brown with red lines on the outer edge of the shell. The fleshy parts of her body had markings of red, black and yellow, and her tail was very short. To Dis, she seemed relatively *unremarkable*, yet just by being in her presence, he strongly sensed something special about her.

"So I understand you wish to be human, Dis, is this true?"

"Oh yes, absolutely...I know it would be wonderful!"

"You really know very little about them...how can you idolize or revere what you know nothing of?" inquired Amee.

"Faith I suppose." answered Dis.

Amee paused for a moment before speaking.

"Faith is a gift and it is an awe-inspiring thing to possess, but you know who you are and you know all who love you. Is that not enough? Why abandon them for your faith into the unknown? If humans are truly as good as you believe, then I know they will eventually come to you with open arms. Be patient and live now the best you can. There is nobility in that. Now is not your time and others depend on you today...*more* than you could possibly realize. But you do have the freedom of choice and I certainly will not stop you. So Dis, I am telling you...once you have your wish granted, there is no power of mine that can change you back. Once you commit...you are committed. It does not get any simpler or more complicated than that."

"I think you already know, I have made my decision ...right or wrong, this is what I desire." Dis said without hesitation.

The *transformation* was almost instantaneous...no fireworks...no pizzazz...in fact the only thing that could be heard was a deadening silence. Dis seemed disorientated for several minutes as his eyes tried to discern a new world that was unfolding in front of him. He was still at the pond, but his vision perceived it quite differently. It was now early morning and his eyesight was not quite as keen as he remembered, his motions seemed slower and his thinking not as crisp. Dis was now human, and in the form of an 85 year old man. He could feel the throbbing pain of arthritis in his hands and knees, his back was humped over, and the thin wrinkly skin that covered his body offered little protection from the early morning cold. Dis could hear the familiar chirping and croaking of his frog friends who were dashing about in the pond under a glowing full moon. He could sense they were searching for him and instantly a feeling of loss and longing covered his feeble body. His voice was too weak to cry out (not that his friends would even understand or recognize him), and oh how he wanted to leap into the still water and meet up with them.

Now a more ominous presence could be seen above Dis, and as he looked up into the night sky, he spotted the familiar figure of a meal-seeking owl circling the pond. As Dis glanced toward the water, his vision for the moment became razor sharp and he could see his best friend, Dat, sitting on a floating branch. Dis could not scream because his voice was so weak, and even if he could, the frogs could now only perceive Dis as a human sitting alongside the pond's edge. He was horrified and all he could do was helplessly watch as the determined owl swooped down in black silence. With perfect execution, Dat was unmercifully snagged in an instant and disappeared into the moon lit sky. Dis' heart sank, and the first human tear slowly rolled down his wrinkled cheek. Nobody knew Dis now...no frogs or humans... there was no home anymore and on this chilly morning, all he could do to stay warm was to pull a discarded newspaper over himself.

A delicate breeze fueled by the cool morning temperatures this summer day quietly passed thru the newspaper covering the old man on the park bench. He was alone in the world...alongside the pond in the middle of the golden meadow.

Ice Time

"Slump? I ain't in no slump. I just ain't hittin."
---Yogi Berra

I could hear the finely tuned metal blades of the skates expertly carve and glide onto the sparkling ice, each sound as crisp and sure as the other. The textbook motion of the hockey player seemed effortless... head up, legs and arms in synchronous harmony... and as the powerful legs churned and sped toward the anxious goalie anticipating his arrival, I could see the icy breath pouring out of the skater's mouth like an *old-time* locomotive smoke stack. With a *Northland Pro* and sure hands gripping the stick, he meticulously guided the black rubber puck as if it were at the end of a string, sliding it from left to right and always skimming forward. The entire scenario seemed as if in *slow motion* because I amazingly could see beads of sweat pour off the skater's tattered chinstrap and fall onto the frosty surface, each droplet exploding on impact with the ice and then freezing in an instant.

All of this activity was occurring in relatively familiar surroundings I thought to myself. There were banners hanging from the rafters of division and conference champions and yes there were banners showing off *Stanley Cup* championships. Although the ice arena I was sitting in wasn't a perfect replica, for all practical purposes, this appeared to be someone's version of *Joe Louis Arena*, home of the *Detroit Red Wing* professional hockey club. There were no plexiglass shields or nets around the rink, the seats surrounding the spacious arena were bleachers that had alternating shades of red and white, and there were no visible exits or entrances I could see except for one. To my right and toward the very top upper edge of the arena were maybe six or seven illuminated steps about four feet long and two feet deep, leading up to two rather (*out of place…mind you)* ornate French doors that had a beautiful rich oak grain, and each door had an elliptical shaped brass handle. At this point in time I also had noticed one of the doors was slightly ajar and a bright light that appeared gold in color pierced thru the narrow opening.

Clearly the *skater* was a determined and competitive hockey player and I was so impressed, I immediately became an active spectator in this mini-spectacle. Nervously, I watched as the skater rushed toward the goalie who was protecting the precious net behind him. I thought the goaltender, who had one of those 1950's style hockey masks with very little padding for protection, would come out of the net to challenge the attack, but instead he calmly remained a foot or two directly in front of the crease. The goalie, I was thinking to myself "*sure looks focused and confident.*" As the skater crossed the blue line, he immediately and without warning raised his stick and with one mammoth downward swoop, the face of the stick paddle violently met the moving puck. It was propelled at a tremendous velocity and as it sped toward its intended target, the goalie wrongly anticipated the screaming missile's direction to his right and had to make an unbelievable leap and lunge to his left where the puck was bearing down. The puck missed the goalie's glove but instead caught him flush on the forehead. The black rubber disk stopped cold, ricocheted off the non-protective mask and fell to the ice harmlessly several feet away from the goal. What a save! I jumped off my uncomfortable bleacher seat and raised my arms with energetic enthusiasm. I guess I was caught up in the moment as it often times happens to me when it comes to sporting events.

"Damn!" shouted the skater in pure disgust and undeniable frustration.

He slammed the wooden stick onto the ice and on impact; splinters were flying everywhere, one catching him on the side of his neck, causing it to bleed. The victorious net minder laughed and for the first time, this distraught hockey player turned toward my direction and peered at me as I was standing on my feet, stupidly jumping up and down and waving my arms.

"Jim, could you please go up there and shut that door…the light is distracting me!" he yelled.

"You have excuses every time I *stone* you," laughed the goalie, "and besides, the light *barely* coming thru that door is behind you, not in front of you! It really shouldn't disturb you at all! Forget about the light and make the shot!"

"Quiet! Would you please?" snorted the player.

I was somewhat startled at the terse command, but just the same, I ran to the top of the arena, up the strangely lit steps, grabbed the brass handle of the slightly opened door and gave it a stiff push so that it would not accidentally open again. Strange, I thought…I ran up a lot of steps to get to the doors, yet I wasn't out of breath as I felt I should have been. I never really was much of an exercise buff and well…I was just plain out of shape. It would not seem so today. Even more peculiar was this stranger…he called me by name and I knew we had never met. As I was about to discover, this was going to be a day of mysteries and profound revelations.

I took a few minutes coming back, but this time I went down to the floor level of the arena where I could lean over the five-foot wall that surrounded the ice rink. My curiosity was peaking *big time* and my *foggy* memory seemed to be clearing up. Where am I? What is this place? I was thinking that I was late for work, but I obviously was nowhere near there now, besides, I…I think I was in some kind of terrible accident! A sharp sensation of pain overcame me at once and as I slid my hand under my *Ferris State University* sweatshirt, I could feel multiple scars on my chest, and my other hand felt for my neck that also had jagged scars. Oddly I felt no fear, but the intense anxiety, wariness and apprehension within me was at an all time high.

"Hey!" I shouted, "Could you please come over here for a moment."

I was embarrassed because I hadn't realized how loud I yelled and the emptiness of the arena just amplified and echoed my bellowing voice. It would appear this time; I was the cause of the player's distraction, because as I hollered at him, he was having another *go at it* with the goalie, and his sizzling shot fizzled helplessly and harmlessly several feet above the cross bar. He made one of those *cool* hockey stops (I could never do), and turned toward me and gave me a stare.

"Look, I spoke rather meekly, I didn't mean to screw up your shot…I'm really sorry."

This time he smiled and said.

"No big deal Jimbo… Terry doesn't beat me all of the time."

"Ha! Don't believe him Jimmy; he only beats me when I let him."

"Hold on! Jim, Jimbo, Jimmy? What am I missing here? Do I know either of you? I'm late for work...no I think I was in this terrible accident...no...that can't be, otherwise I would probably be dead!" I spoke in total confusion.

"Bingo!" shouted the goaltender named Terry, "You know Mr.G... it always takes them some time before they figure it out."

Apparently this hockey player with the errant shot was Mr.G. Now I felt I was getting somewhere.

"Dead? What do you mean...are you implying I'm dead?"

"Oh, don't listen to Terry. Do you look dead? Do you feel dead? Let's just say you're not where you *used to be* and now you're here where you *are supposed to be*. Make sense?" Mr.G said looking right at me.

I was now finally face to face with this imposing man. He was all of 6 foot 2 inches and even with his hockey gear on I could tell that he must have weighed in at about 210...all muscle. He pulled off his helmet and looked directly at me. His features were rather ordinary, with eyes that appeared to me almost sad looking, hazel green in color and his lips and mouth seemed to hide a reluctant and uneasy sort of smile. He also sported a short trimmed black beard, the weave only interrupted by two scars on his chin. In theme with the surroundings, this Mr.G was wearing a *Detroit Red Wing* jersey with a conspicuous capital letter *G* on the left front shoulder, a location generally reserved for the letter *C* for captain, or *A* for assistant captain. Sweat was rolling profusely from his head on down causing his jersey to be pretty well drenched. I looked at him…he stared thru me like a laser and needless to say this first encounter with Mr.G was interesting and full of unanswered questions.

"Hey! Mr.G, I'm going to get this forehead of mine stitched up and then take a long hot shower," hollered Terry.

"Go on *tough guy*, but I'll get that puck past you tomorrow! You'll see! Ha! Ha!"

"It was nice meeting you Jimmy. Maybe you could give this old guy a pointer (*yeah…right!*) or two because I think he needs more help than his pride will admit to!" Spoke Terry jokingly.

Terry was laughing hard as he headed down the tunnel in the arena. Hmm…I hadn't noticed that before. It was now just the two of us in the quiet arena…I presumed, but this obviously was no ordinary day and up near the lit doorsteps was another figure heading toward the direction of the two doors. Funny observation…when I was up there closing the door, it had a brass handle, but now as I could plainly see the handles on either door were no longer there, but instead they were flat with no apparent way of opening them. The figure turned toward us and what do you know…it was someone I did recognize! It was the man (*ugh! now I remember*) who was on the hood of my smashed automobile. He looked at me first and then spoke.

"Howdy senor Jeem!"

He smiled his Mona Lisa grin at me as he did (*unceremoniously*) before and then focused on Mr.G the hockey player.

"Hasta manana, senor G!"

Mr.G waved to him, "Hasta manana my friend Diego!"

Diego gave us a half wave, turned his back to us and as if on cue, the doors opened wide and a miraculous showering warm light rushed into the arena. I had been to a *Pink Floyd* concert before, but I can tell you, this was a light show like no other. A feeling of euphoria, warmth and peace swelled in my body and needless to say it was beyond incredible. I could see Diego enter into the light, the doors then gently closed and once again to my surprise, the two brass handles appeared as I had originally seen them. Now for sure, we were alone.

"This day is turning into a total *weird-out* for me, Mr.G…it is Mr.G, I presume?"

He paused for a moment. While I generally say what is on my mind in quick spontaneity, it would seem this

Mr.G thought things over a bit before he would speak, even for the simplest inquires.

"Mr.G is ok," he said in a quiet and thoughtful manner…"Jim ok with you?"

"Sure, that's me, Jim," I spoke with an incredulous tone in my voice.

It was almost as if I didn't believe who I was and my response to this Mr.G was at best apprehensive.

"You are obviously and understandably disorientated, Jim…so is there anything I can say or do to help clear the air for you?"

"*Help me Rhonda*! That's an understatement!" I blurted out.

"*Beach Boys*? Right?"

"What? Oh yeah, right. Sure, you can definitely try to help me make sense of this incredibly crazy kind of day I am having. I was going to work…I think I was in a rather horrible auto accident…I apparently was in this wreck with that Diego fellow who just disappeared past those doors, and if I am not mistaken…what Terry inferred…is it possible I'm dead!? If I am dead, what is this place and who are you?" I spoke in one frenzied rapid-fire breath.

Mr.G spoke.

"Your first point, yes you were going to work, point two…did you ever consider reading your mail instead of sticking it onto the refrigerator and forgetting about it?

Hello! If you read it, you would have known you had a problem with your car and you would not have been in that tragic accident. Point three...Diego was most definitely the driver in the 18-wheeler. Point four, this is *Joe Lewis Arena*...you've already figured that out."

"Ok, right! This is not *Joe Louis Arena* and you really didn't answer the two most important questions."

The tone of my voice was now more forceful and demanding as I was just not in the mood for anymore guessing games. Mr.G could see the fire in my eyes and feel the urgency in my manner. Again he seemed to stare right thru me and spoke.

"Who do you think I am?"

"Hell if I know...maybe nobody! This is probably just a dream anyway, although I must admit, if it is, it's by far the most graphic and most intense. So my answer to you is I really don't have a clue and I don't care! Now, I suppose you're going to tell me you're *God*! Right?"

He started laughing...loud enough, so that the entire building echoed with his voice, bouncing off the ceiling and walls. It was as if there were thousands of people in the ice arena.

"What's so funny? Is this a joke? You sure seem awfully amused," I spoke with a tone of irritation.

"Really Jim, I apologize, it's just the way you said *hell*," he chuckled.

Again he spoke.

"Look, you said you don't have a clue, yet in the next breath you said "*now I suppose you're going to tell me you're God! Right?*" I think I quoted you word for word on that."

He gave me a friendly smile and in an instant, he was skating again. The ice became his canvas and the artistic skills he possessed were just amazing as he glided and performed figure eights over and over again each time going exactly over the identical spot he skated on before. He flung his gloves into the frigid air and looked up to the ceiling shouting like a madman.

"Jim, who am I…who am I…who am I!?"

Now I started laughing as I watched this grown macho guy skating and looking silly as he shouted his question at me.

"I think you might be one crazy dude, Mr.G, that's who I think you are."

Once again he skated toward me and did an exaggerated hockey stop causing the shavings of ice to spray onto my face. For a moment, I calmed down and just laughed.

"Jim, I really think you know who I am, and you just won't say it because if you do, then you will know the answer to the question you really don't want to ask or have answered."

"But…but you said I wasn't dead! Didn't you?"

"No, I said and I quote, *"do you look dead…do you feel dead?"*

"Oh, this is just great! This ticks me off! I am dead and apparently the *G* on your jersey does stand for *God*! I suppose I'm in big trouble now, right?"

"Hmm….I thought the *G* was for GREAT…as in great hockey player." Spoke Mr.G.

Mr.G again thought before he spoke.

"You know I really don't care for the word *dead*, Jim…because it's too permanent. Existence is a long process, certainly longer than 50 years…much longer than a thousand years. Why do you think you're in some kind of trouble? Do I look like some kind of *judge* to you?"

"I'll be honest, Mr.G, I just don't know what to think."

"Jim, why don't you just sit down and relax. A gift is being offered to you. Why don't we just get to know each other and talk. Fair enough?"

I looked at him and said, "Sure, why not."

"Strength does not come from physical capacity. It comes from an indomitable will."
---Mahatma Gandhi

The Gardner

"Joy is not in things! It is in us!"
---Benjamin Franklin

Nevaeh (nay-va) was a wondrous world to live in. As the sun would rise in the early morning, soft and gentle rays of light would permeate thru all the living things of this magical paradise and regenerate the very essence of life within them. Pleasant warm breezes, the enticing scent of lilac and wisteria, and restful sounds of ice cold water dancing over the smooth rocks in the brook, gave this place a feeling of wonder and tranquility. This Nevaeh was indeed a land of plenty. Trees of redwood, oak and maple would ascend to the clouds and quietly whisper each other's secrets as the mellow winds swirled thru their hardy branches and fluttering leaves. Animals small and large alike would share this Eden together in respectful friendship and play all day long beside the river and throughout the lush plants and flowers that completely enveloped the landscape.

The Gardner was a man of few words and bold actions. He was the one responsible for overseeing and nurturing the land of Nevaeh. His abilities to plant and tend for the flowers, fruits and vegetables of this world were truly remarkable. Each day he would toil in the fields and see to it that every plant in his domain was cared for in the manner that was needed in order for them to thrive and survive. The Gardner would spare nothing of his efforts when it came to his plants and because of this extraordinary diligence, the land of Nevaeh remained stunning and pristine.

But all was not perfect, as it would seem...for the Gardner was the only one of his kind in Nevaeh. He was alone and this life of isolation made him longing for companionship.

On this particular morning there was a gentle rain falling, each raindrop gleefully sliding off the wax-coated leaves of the many plants and trees, and then playfully falling onto the rich black soil. The Gardner was moving the ground beneath him and gently caressing a seedling as he buried it into the earth's fertile womb. This, he imagined to himself would be a *spectacular* sunflower, and soon, it would rise magnificently toward the sky and literally capture the rays of the sun. It was a miracle to witness and his pleasure showed with a broad smile and a twinkle in his eyes. It would seem like a typical morning in Nevaeh...but it wasn't.

The Gardner knew how to converse with the other creatures of this land and so it came to be, on this morning, a chirping robin was describing to the Gardner of a land not so far in the distance that was inhabited by creatures of his likeness! How could this be? Immediately he set out to explore this unknown hidden region and seek out others like him. This would be wonderful! He could hardly contain his excitement!

Following the directions of the robin and after a few days of travel, the Gardner came to the top of a very tall hill overlooking a land that seemed so different to him. In the distance he could see distinct congregations of beings like himself, but the ground around them was barren. There were only a few leafless trees and the terrain was rough, rocky and arid. This he learned was the land of Namuh (nay-moo).

"And why is this world so void of life?" Inquired the Gardner to the first stranger he met.

"The ground beneath us is cursed!" Said the stranger in disgust.

"Cursed? How can this be? Would you let me stay with your people? I will show you how to make your land come alive as you have never seen before…I am the Gardner.

The stranger cautiously agreed and within months, the Gardner was able to have the people of the village agree to his methods of invigorating the very land they thought of as bedeviled. Within a very short period of time, this particular village in the land of Namuh was transformed into a lush paradise brimming with life and energy. The instructions of the Gardner were followed by all and to the amazement of the people; they witnessed wonders they thought impossible. After a good deal of strenuous work and sweat, they were reaping the rewards with bountiful harvests of fruits and vegetables, the soil became enriched and the flowers and trees took root and burst toward the azure sky. Although the Gardner's method of reviving this tiny village was a bit different than the way he kept his land of Nevaeh, his basic premise for success was the same...*caring, nurturing and love*. The Gardner was pleased and remained in the village; after all, he finally had the companionship of friends who loved him.

Unfortunately it didn't take long before some people decided to make their own rules and devise their own methods. Inner squabbles became common amongst the people and this ultimately festered into dissension within the village. The people became disillusioned...little by little the basic premise of the Gardner became lost, and while some citizens were able to hold onto the Gardner's lessons, many discarded them. It was becoming all too evident as parcels of land again became barren and bereft of life. Sadly the people continued to fight and lose sight of their own common sense. The Gardner would try to steer the people back on the steady and sure path, but even he could not convince all. In fact, there were some very convincing *preachers* who said they spoke for the Gardner and persuaded many to believe things that simply were not the truth. This made the Gardner painfully anguished and after a few more agonizing months, he decided to depart and travel to another village.

In this new village, the Gardner found himself in circumstances very similar to the one he had just left. This time however, he decided that maybe a different approach might be the remedy to correct what went wrong in the past. The one thing he did know was that he could not change the basic premise of *caring, nurturing and love.* This was a mainstay that simply could not be altered. Alas, it didn't take very long when the same troubles occurred. The Gardner as before traveled again to another village and another, each time trying a new method for the people with the *basic premise* being the same, but sadly… the results were all too predictable. Finally there were no more villages left and so with much regret and a heavy heart, the Gardner decided to return to where he had been at the beginning…Nevaeh.

"I had to leave," sighed the Gardner to his robin friend. "I gave the people the secret for their success…

they have it and they know it...now it is up to them... not me, to do what is right."

In the distance, the Gardner and robin could now clearly see the many villages that they hadn't seen before. The sounds of bickering, fighting and hatred were abound. Each village declared they were doing the wishes of the Gardner, but most of them really didn't have a clue.

"I think it will be a long time before they come around," said the robin.

"I am afraid you are probably right," cried the Gardner.

"You can judge the character of a man by how he treats those who can do nothing for him."---James D. Miles

...on the Doorsteps of Heaven

"To declare yourself politically correct in essence is to say you have no opinion of your own."
---j.j. Giordano

"A gift, you said, right?"

"Yes...yes...Jimmy...that is correct," Mr.G said playfully with his eyes rolling.

I know I had somewhat agreed to sit back and relax, but I just couldn't help myself and my anxiety was peaking.

"Honestly, Mr.G, I really don't comprehend. Here I find myself in *Joe Louis Arena*...which is *Heaven*? Gee, who thought of that? I'm swearing *hell* and *shit*, only to realize that I am speaking with the creator himself. I also had to DIE to get here! (Duh...what other way is there to get to *Heaven*?) It would have been a lot simpler to just purchase a ticket from *Ticket Master*. I'd bet my seats would have been better too!"

Now, this Mr.G is roaring with laughter, harder than ever, while he's watching me vent my frustrations and tensions.

"Do you always rant like this? You're hilarious, especially seeing the way your baldhead turns beet red and how your arms and hands flail about like you had a jolt of electricity. But let me AGAIN answer your litany of questions. Like I said, this is the *JLA* and by the way, this very cool arena was my idea! The JLA...is almost *Heaven*...let's just say for your understanding...pre-*Heaven*. Secondly, you did say hell, but never SHIT, (he really emphasized that!), and to me, those words are just your way of making a point or blowing off steam. No big deal. Thirdly, yes in a way I am a creator, but maybe not necessarily the way most people think. You also keep insisting that you are dead, but Jim, I just don't see it that way. Look at yourself... you're breathing, sweating...and YOU'RE HUNGRY!!! I completely forgot my manners. Sorry. How can you think or converse on an empty stomach?"

In a New York minute, I found Mr.G and myself seated in what would seem to be a typical traditional Italian restaurant. The lights were dim, the tablecloths were red and white checker, the large bottle of wine to the side of us was *Fortissimo*...room temperature, dark red and dry. The aroma of garlic, oregano, basil, and pungent *Fontinella* cheese filled the room, and in the background you could hear the music of an accordion player singing, (of course in Italian). A short skinny waiter, black hair, brown eyes, handlebar mustache, and a large nose promptly brought several dishes of steaming rigatoni marinara, baked ziti (with a *Parmigiano-Reggiano* sauce), sweet Italian fennel sausage and fresh bread to our table. Mr. G, now in blue jeans, was still wearing his *Red Wing* jersey. He reached for his cloth napkin and tucked it into his jersey, just below his chin. Since I figured that I really might be having dinner with God, I decided to follow suit.

"So tell me Mr.G, if this is not quite *Heaven*, something tells me it can't be too far away. Right? Where is it? And just an observation…pre-*Heaven* or *Heaven*, I always thought once you attained eternal life, there was no need for food…in fact you would never be hungry to begin with. Now…I'm hungry and it sure looks as if you are too!"

Mr.G, as I was getting used to, took his time and I could see the wheels spinning in his head…besides the large portion of pasta in his mouth really did not allow him to speak. He reached for his napkin, wiped some tomato sauce from his mouth and beard, set his fork down and spoke.

"Hunger? Let me ask you. When you're hungry, like now, and you dig into that "*Heavenly"* ziti, followed by a warm heal of fresh Italian bread, how much enjoyment do you have? And conversely, let's say you ate, even though you weren't hungry at all. Would the pleasure or level of satisfaction be the same?"

"Well in most instances, I suppose, you really can only enjoy food if you're hungry," I spoke.

"So you see Jim, you answered one of your questions. Food in *Heaven*, and by the way you just can't beat it...food in *Heaven* is obviously not for survival, but for enjoyment...and therefore...

I interjected...

"You need to have hunger."

The meal was quite incredible and I wasn't shy about seconds. Mr.G joined in and we toasted our glasses of wine to a new friendship. This was actually quite fun and for awhile...just awhile, I forgot about my questions and tried to relax with this very interesting man.

"*Heaven*, you still haven't told me where this place is. You can't fault me for wondering."

"Jim, did you know this multiverse has "*billions and billions*" of possibilities?" spoke Mr.G in his best Carl Sagan. "*Heaven* is truly just another beginning, not an end...and guess what? It really is not the most significant part of the journey!"

He spoke with an excitement that you see when someone is just about to tell you something *very cool*. His eyes bugged out, his motions exaggerated as his arms and hands were bouncing about, looking like a marionette at the end of strings. Funny...he talked with his hands much the same way my wife MJ did. If you tied her hands, I swear she would probably be mute!........... I responded.

"So Earth is in a universe, *Heaven* is in its own universe and beyond *Heaven* there are more universes? I did catch multiverse, although I think you just invented the word. How am I doing so far?"

"Not bad for a 1st day guy."

I asked the question…again.

"Ok, so where is it…*Heaven*?

Mr.G laughed.

"You were right there!" He smiled, "RIGHT THERE! You, Jimbo, not too very long ago were …on the doorsteps of *Heaven*!"

Frankly I didn't know whether to be excited or disappointed. All I knew was that I felt a sudden rush of adrenalin; my feet were like ice, my stomach knotted up; there was sweat on my palms and my face turned flush. Mr.G sure seemed interested in my reactions and didn't say anything; he just sat and stared at me.

I spoke.

"Mr.G, our mutual amigo, Diego, he went to *Heaven*…right? Yeah, up those steps and beyond those curious doors with the disappearing and reappearing brass handles. The doorsteps of *Heaven*! Whadda ya know! All I had to do was open the doors…and…"

"...And you would have been there...Yep! Yep! Yep...Jimmy Jimbo is now entering the great heavens... hurry, hurry, and get your tickets! Isn't life grand! It's marvelous! It's "*supercalifragilisticexpialidodous*"! You never really know from one second to another how your world within you or around you can change so quickly and dramatically. This is what makes the journey so rewarding! Life is "*like a box of chocolates*"..."

"...ok...ok...Mr.G, I get the point. You're watching too many movies. Speaking of journeys, you mentioned that going to *Heaven* is not really the most crucial part of this whole deal. So what is it?"

"Well Jim, I sort of jumped the gun on that one. I will give you the answer, but not right now. I have my reasons, and well, you'll just have to trust me on this one. Ok?"

"So have a little *faith* in you?" I asked.

"Now that was funny!" Mr.G said laughing.

"Look," I said, "I'm embarrassed. I admit I spent a good part of my life not believing in you and the word *faith* was rarely in my vocabulary. Now you're asking this of me?"

"I just said *trust*, Jim, but I will also have something to tell you about faith and how it ties in with your special journey. Be patient and you will know. As I said, for now Jim, just *trust* me."

"Ok, who's to argue with God? I said.

"You are Jim! I love disagreements and arguments and differences of opinion. This is how you learn and grow. You can only be who you are! You need to be able to think for yourself and be different, because you are different! That's the way it's supposed to be. Variety truly is the *spice of life*, and differences mean change and change can be a very *good thing.*"

"And if it isn't? I asked.

"Well then you try something else man! If you don't like anchovies does that mean you give up on eating? You know what's funny…all of this *stuff* is common sense and I know you've always been big on common sense. Right, Jim?"

"Yes, but I just left a world where in most instances, if you had common sense, it would make no sense at all."

"Sure, like political correctness?" Jumped in Mr.G.

"Oh God yeah!" I said.

"Hey, this is fun, Jim. The conversation, the food…I knew this would be an interesting meeting. How about an almond biscotti and some espresso?"

"Sounds terrific, Mr.G".

"Jim, the reason for political correctness, is because it's a way for a dominant group to make decisions concerning entire ideas on how to think or literally how to live one's life. It doesn't really allow you to have your own thoughts or ideas because if you cross the line, then you're out of the club; you're chastised and abandoned. It is someone thinking for you...a form of control... and that isn't a *good thing*. I am well aware some forms of conformity are necessary to maintain order in cultures, but your world Jim, has taken it to a new level. This is not an example of common sense. *Lemmings*, Jim, *lemmings*! You know all about those politically correct mammals, one by one all jumping to their deaths."

"Ah yes, *lemmings*...into the abyss," I quietly said to myself.

Mr.G was on a roll. He enjoyed talking and probably loved the sound of his voice.

"What about believing in you Mr.G...or getting to Heaven? Those certainly can be *p.c.* issues. Do you think so?"

I looked at Mr.G and was ultimately curious as to his reaction and answers to my questions.

"Hmmmmmm...I guess...if someone believes in God for show or convenience or maybe because it's the popular thing to do... then I'd say it's a flawed concept. As far as Heaven goes...too many people eye the prize of eternal life and see God as their ticket and while they're obsessed about *Heaven*, they should be more attentive about what they are doing with their lives right now, on Earth. You know...I was never meant to be a distraction.

So Terry was right," I said.

"Terry?"

Mr.G looked confused.

"Remember, Mr.G, he said forget about the light and make the shot. Didn't he?"

He made a childish face at me, realizing the analogy.

"So now you know...God isn't perfect," he shot back.

"Not to sound too arrogant, but I never really ever thought if there was a God...that he would be perfect. Now I believe ... and you pretty much have confirmed what I have always suspected. Do you think you should be perfect? Is it important to you? Of course a great deal of believers think you are the absolute picture of perfection, but that shouldn't dishearten you because you're not. Honestly, I'm more comfortable with you when you ask me questions and you're not sure of my answers! That makes your questions relevant and not something just for your amusement. My answer means something to you. Seriously, Mr.G, look at the world I just left...the misery, the hatred, the lost hope...it's all around and it started at the very beginning...I presume, and I suspect it will continue until humanity itself has disappeared. Does that sound like a world a *perfect* being would create? I don't think so and I really don't give a *hoot*. Like you said, I am a common sense kind of guy."

It was almost as if a load had been lifted off his shoulders. This heavy burden he was carrying seemed to melt away like a pad of butter on a hot skillet. This was a very good man I was speaking with and whatever barriers we may have had between the two of us...disappeared.

"Do you dislike or hold it against atheists or agnostics for their non-belief or skepticism? Would they be in a *heap of trouble* with you?"

"I told you before...I am not a judge. Well I may be, sort of, but I'll get back to you on that also. To your question, Jim, no...why would I dislike someone because they don't believe I exist? Look at you, you're having a meal with me and you've swayed back and forth like a pendulum your entire life with this issue. Look...it's difficult to believe in someone or something you have never seen. I really do understand...it's no big deal! I will say, it is comforting to know that there are believers...makes me feel...alive! ...and your parents, Jim, now they believe in me, no questions asked. That is special and rare. You're lucky to have a wonderful Mom and Dad. I think they're terrific and someday I will personally tell them. I also promise to take them out to this very restaurant and I assure you, your Father's soup and espresso will be steaming hot and your Mother's wine will have an ice cube in it!"

We sat for maybe another half hour and just relaxed and enjoyed the silence. It was a comfortable silence.

Neither of us talked as we sipped the aromatic espresso and quietly relished the moments we were spending together. Funny…it would seem…Mr.G himself was a *lonely fellow*, and my company and our friendly banter, uplifted his spirits. Who would have thought?

"Imagine," I said in an almost whisper. "…on the doorsteps of *Heaven*."

"Yes-er-ee-bob…you were right there, Jim…right there."

> *"Political, social, moral or religious correctness often times*
> *are artificial truths that control the freedom of thought and*
> *views of non-artificial people."*
> *---j.j.Giordano*

Significance

"If you can't feed a hundred people, then feed just one."
---Mother Teresa

So where did you come from?" I inquired, staring directly at Mr.G

The meal and conversation was exceptional and shortly afterward, we got up and headed toward a door at the rear of the restaurant. I was beginning to realize (duh!) that my private audience with God was quite extraordinary and with this acknowledgement, I could only anxiously wait to see what was going to happen next. We stepped outside to a very large field stone patio that had an oak railing surrounding it. The patio overlooked a splendid lush valley, a swift moving river and a ruggedly beautiful mountain range that soared to the heavens; no pun intended. It appeared to be a typical summer afternoon; warm temperatures, a slight and soothing breeze and in the sky were two suns; clearly smaller than the one I knew of on Earth, but without a doubt, unbelievably breathtaking. I could peer directly at these shining objects without blinking or covering my eyes, yet the light they shed on the valley was brilliantly bright…and the colors! The colors of these incredible fire balls seemed to vary at every look; first a dazzling yellow-orange to a blazing red, and then they would shimmer to a soft blue haze. Needless to say, it was mesmerizing and resplendent. We didn't say anything for quite sometime, although I could sense Mr.G was more than interested in my reactions to these strange and new surroundings. Eventually, I turned toward him and asked the question.

"Where did I come from?" Spoke Mr.G, posing a question to my question.

"Yeah, how did you come to be? It's hard to imagine you *always were and always will be* as I was taught, yet the events of today I am witnessing are making me realize… maybe anything is possible."

"Honestly, I really don't know," Answered Mr.G.

"That's your answer? This is your answer to one of the most important mysteries of all time? You say, "I really don't know?" Please Mr.G, say it ain't so!!"

"Jim, you aren't the only one on this wonderful journey of life. I too am searching like you are. You sensed my loneliness very shortly after we met. Look, however I came to be, it would appear the mold was broken and I am the only one. I am a man, as you can see, but it's obvious my unique abilities, if you will, definitively separate me from others. Don't misunderstand…it's not that I am unhappy…because I'm not…it's just there are times when I long for answers to mysteries that I cannot solve."

"Mysteries? Like where you came from?" I asked.

"Right," Mr.G said in a quiet voice.

"Well Mr.G, do any of the thousands of religions have it right about you? There was a time when I wasn't smashing into 18-wheelers, and in that time, I witnessed the way religions were the ones crashing into one another. Do you know what I mean?"

"Most religions do have it right. Surprised? It's the bureaucracy in religions that get in the way. They become arrogant…self-righteous…with feelings of superiority and these misguided thoughts blind them to the truth. Why do you think there are so many conflicts? Energies are misdirected to ideas that simply have nothing to do with God, or *Heaven*, or salvation…or eternal life. Jim, I know you understand the difference between right and wrong; good and evil. Right? Sure you do! It's really that simple. Unfortunately everyone wants to have the *right* God and say they are the *chosen* ones. How silly! They really have no idea how uncomplicated I can be. They don't get it…they don't have a clue! Do I really look like I want to be a king or a ruler of some utopian kingdom? Frankly most people despise or are in fear of their rulers, kings and dictators. I would never want you to think of me that way. I truthfully don't require worship or adoration, but what I desire is what everyone else truly craves…and that is love…unconditional love. Pretty simple? Yes?

"Sounds simple enough, yeah, but why then is it so difficult? It's not as if this *uncomplicated* approach hasn't been proclaimed many times over, but a lot of people just can't get it right. Hell, I never could get it right!"

"That, Jim, is because *you're* not perfect! Life is a series of mistakes and retakes; you make an error, hopefully learn from it and then you go back and try all over again. If you didn't make mistakes, you could never learn. It's all part of the game of life; you play with the hand dealt to you and make the best of it…or you don't. Living the first part of your life is not an easy journey and while it is mere microseconds in the timetable of your universe, your trek on Earth is the *most significant.*"

"Huh, this is the second time you've mentioned that, but you've never really expounded on it. So if you please, Mr.G, and unless this information is classified top secret, please share with me your thoughts on mankind's journey on Earth. What is my journey?"

I suppose by now, I should have at least half expected something to happen in an extraordinary way, but I didn't…and it did! *Star Trek* was my absolute favorite and it always amazed me at the unusual and unique ideas that *Gene Roddenberry* and his fellow producers/writers would come up with for their television series and motion pictures. *"Beam me up Scottie"*, or something close to that, was a rather famous line in the *Star Trek* series that described the process of having a person's atoms and molecules scrambled in an energy form and then having them transported from one place to another in a matter of seconds. This unparalleled form of travel could take a person or objects in an instant to a predetermined destination sometimes light years away. Once you reached that destination, your energy form would be unscrambled and you would be *put back together* again. Needless to say, it was a very *cool* way to travel...and it also disproved the *Humpty Dumpty* theory!

Mr.G never said *"beam me up"* or *"energize"*, but in a blink of an eye, lickity split, I found Mr.G and myself on a large wooden four-mast schooner in the middle of an ocean. Although I didn't see anybody at the helm, this handsomely sleek ship seemed to be in absolute control as it cruised rapidly across the open blue water, cutting thru large and small waves alike with perfect ease. Above, the deep purple-blue sky was sporadically occupied by flocks of creamy white clouds racing and dancing with the steady and firm motion of the wind. The two suns I had witnessed not long ago were shining brightly, dispersing a gentle and soothing warm sensation that seemed to massage my entire body. Funny…I could hear thousands of sounds…the wind, the billowing sails, the waves crashing and churning, the creaking of the ship, and yet everything in my mind was silent and at peace. My soul was content even beyond my wildest imaginations. If this wasn't *Heaven*, then it should have been.

My *spiritual* calm was abruptly halted by the sound of a hard-driving 1960's style melody. It was in the genre of surf music, originally made popular by the *Beach Boys* and *Jan and Dean.*

Where the music came from, I couldn't really tell you, except that it seemed to blanket the entire area. Immediately I recognized the song… **Wave**, a tune my oldest son Chris composed. My wife MJ and I used to go to some of the local pubs and cafes to watch Chris and his band perform. It was loads of fun because he always had a large group of friends come out…and with them we would have a few beers and a great time listening to the talents of this gifted unassuming musician. Although there were no vocals to the song, the crisp melody from Chris's electric guitar screamed of passion and high energy. As if on cue, no more than a hundred yards or so off the port bow of the ship were dozens of young men and women surfing these wild waves to the intense pulse of the music. It was a peculiar site to observe, but exhilarating at the same time. I guess you could say it was just plain fun!

"You listen to his music all of the time, Jim," spoke Mr.G, as we were watching the surfers skim and skip across wave after wave.

"Yes, I do," I said.

"Of course you couldn't possibly know, but I am a big fan of his music. When I see Chris creating sounds that blend into such perfection, it really is quite thrilling to me. You must know how important music is to him and the passion he has for it is so strong and true. At first it was difficult for you and MJ, but you did the right thing in never discouraging him concerning his music. I guess when you and MJ went into the *huddle*; you both called the *right play*...no fumbles on that possession! He will do wonderful things with his talents...you just wait and see. Inventive and creative ideas like music, humor and good conversation are things I find intriguing. Did you ever notice the wonderful subtle humor your Andrew has, or how deeply he thinks when talking about a subject he's really into? As far as his spontaneous humor goes, it astounds me at how he can come up with ideas that simply make me laugh and at the same time you can approach him with a serious subject matter and he genuinely will give you a well thought out observation or answer. You wouldn't know he is only 17 years old. Bottom line...Jim...your children are special."

"My two sons…yeah…special, aren't they?

I spoke quietly, looking out at nothing with a blank and far away expression.

"Yes, Jim, you're fortunate…and I know you know that."

For several minutes there was a silence between the two of us as we looked out across the vastness of the ocean. The music disappeared and the surfers vanished. Now it was just the sound of the wind, the waves and the sailboat ever rocking and pushing along.

"Jim, did you know your Earth is about 4.5 billion years old and human beings didn't arrive on Earth until much later? In fact to make it easy to understand, think of the history of Earth as a single day. Dinosaurs don't even appear until the late evening hours and humans just arrive very shortly before midnight. Your civilization doesn't even come into play until less than a second before midnight! What does that tell you about your relationship with mankind and all that is in it? What is the *significance* to this?"

"Mr.G, I don't know what you are getting at."

Mr.G immediately went down on his knees and started to patiently smooth his right hand…palm down, over the harsh wooden surface of the schooner. I'm now asking myself, "*What is he doing?*"

"Ouch! Damn!" shouted Mr.G as he pulled his hand to his chest.

"What's the problem?" I asked.

"I caught a sliver in my hand. It's amazing *how such a tiny piece of wood can cause so much pain.*"

He bent over again and continued his search for *whatever* he was searching for.

"Ah, there you are Jim! Trying to hide from me.?"

What? Now I was perplexed. Here I'm intently observing God searching for *who knows what* on the deck of this ship, only to see him pick up what would appear to be one tiny grain of sand and then carry on a conversation with it! Oh, well, he did say he liked conversation.

"Are you ok Mr.G?" I inquired.

"I'm perfectly fine, Jimbo. Why do you ask?"

"Oh, it was just I couldn't help but overhear you talking to that grain of sand you have between your thumb and forefinger. Am I missing something here?"

"Hmmm...thumb...forefinger.... Huh...what an odd comment...you think? Anyway, this grain of sand Jim...is YOU!"

"Me?"

"No, not me...YOU!"

"You?" I asked again.

"No, Jim, I'm being serious. This unassuming little pebble is YOU!!

"Gee, I never looked so good," I spoke in a rather sarcastic monotone voice.

79

He laughed, looked at me and spoke.

"Yes, this seemingly insignificant grain of sand is you. Come over here to the side of the ship with me. I want to show you something that should peak your interest and curiosity."

He glanced towards me to be certain I had his full attention, and then reeled back as if he were *Cy Young* and threw that grain of sand overboard into the swirling winds. It was a rather peculiar, yet rousing event to witness because everything in my view seemed to slow down quite dramatically. I could clearly see the grain tossing and gyrating to the will of the blowing wind, only to be eventually pulled down by the natural force of gravity as it headed for the surface of the water.

"You see Jim; it is this unalterable instant in time… the moment you were thrown into the endless churning ocean of life…you came to be! A nanosecond sooner, a microsecond later, a different place, or a different time… well it really doesn't matter except it wouldn't have been you, but someone else. It is this precise moment in time that only you could possess, where the creation of your spirit, your soul, came to exist. *Exist*…yes Jim; you are the living dynamic spirit…unique for all time. You *are and always will be.* Sound familiar? How exhilarating… how so very cool! Watch! This is only the beginning, Jim. Splash! You've just made impact with the water.

Kind of cold, huh? There you go! Look, Jim, see the waves pushing and tossing you about…and feel that strong tropical current caressing you, as you make your decent to the ocean floor. This is how it happens to all of humanity, except each time it's different and unique to that individual person. We are the same yet so indisputably a one of a kind! It always astounds me…no it blows me away how life is so beautiful and unpredictable! Well, it looks like you're in for a soft landing…and…holy cow!… look at the two grains of sand you fell in between!"

"Who?" I asked with much anticipation.

"Your parents of course, who do you think you would settle next to?"

"Ok," I said. "Right."

"This is your beginning and it is the only way it could have happened. Look at all those pebbles around you. Recognize them?"

"I'm not…not…"

"Sure you do Jim! There are your brothers, Joe, Mike and David, your sister Claire, your two sons, Mary Jane, relatives, friends and the millions of people that share the planet with you. All of these grains of sand are part of you! *Significance*! That saying about this being a *small world*, Jim, certainly rings true. Don't you think? Remember, I said you arrived here less than a second before midnight. Now, do you get it?"

"Yeah, I think so…I…"

Interrupted again.

"Jim, let's examine these grains of sand around you even more. Ok? See this smooth lavender colored grain? That is a boy named Isha. He lives in Africa and is suffering horribly and will soon face an excruciating death due to AIDS. Thankfully, he will be visiting me shortly. That green pebble is Sonya. She is a prisoner in a sweatshop in the former Soviet Union…her life is in a state of constant misery and hopelessness. Look here…this large group. They've been dumped in mass graves in Iraq…all because of a ruthless dictator whose sociopathic behavior displayed no value for human life. In fact, there is that dictator, Jim. You know, he really is not far from where you lie. Oh boy, there's Chuck Taylor of Omaha, Nebraska. He's a CEO of a very large corporation, and without any remorse or caring, he steals retirement money by the bundle from the very people that work for him! Those unlucky persons trust him. Did you notice, they are but a few inches away from you? This grain is Emily Harrison. She lives in a rat-infested project with her 3 children in your hometown of Detroit. She tries to make ends meet, but there is little hope… nobody cares! She's desperate and has turned to selling drugs in order for her family to survive. A few miles from the Harrison dwelling, Jake Stone is having the time of his life. Jake is wealthy and right now he's at the casino, gambling away a lot of money. No problem for Jake, he has plenty of dough! Wow! This is your world Jim! See that homeless man sleeping on the park bench…he once was somebody's son, somebody's Father… husband… employee…somebody's friend. He's alone and there's no one willing to befriend or comfort him. Lot's of lonely people in the world, Jim…where are the kind words… where is the compassion? Hmmmm…does Tim Clark ring a bell with you Jim… It should?"

"No, Mr.G, I can't say it does."

"You should, because he's pretty close to you. Maybe if you saw a photograph of him…then you might remember?"

Mr.G showed me a black and white of a boy, maybe 13 or 14 years old…his face seemed pale and sad. In an instant, I felt flush! I did know him…it was around 1965 or 1966, when…as a teenager, I happened to be coming out of a Catholic religious education class and one of my friends pointed to a young boy (about our age), who also was walking out of the school building. We had discovered, this particular boy, Tim Clark, had a Father who happened to be in prison, and our *guilt by association* mentality led us to believe that this Tim must also be some kind of no good idiot. We were the idiots. There were four of us and just him, so we decided to give him a hard time.

"Your Father is a jail bird!" We would yell.

He was obviously vulnerable and we took full advantage of the situation. After several minutes of unforgiving and tasteless verbal abuse, we stopped and just laughed at him. I stared at him and at that moment, I saw a poor helpless kid, alone and unable to defend himself. He was hurt and embarrassed…his head was down and I could see tears rolling down his cheeks. We were so heartless! How did it ever get to this point? Why were we acting in this cruel manner?

He proceeded to walk at a faster pace away from us and as far as we were concerned, the fun was over …so we headed home. I mentioned to my buddies that I had left something behind at school and therefore had to go back. They left and I stayed. Looking the other way down the street, I spotted this poor beaten up boy and decided to try and catch up with him and tell him how sorry I was. Unfortunately, I stopped in my tracks because my fear and pride got in the way of having me do the right thing. I still think about this boy I humiliated and I wished I could have told him how sorry I was, and how so terribly wrong I was.

"Interesting, Jim…it's amazing *how just a few unkind words can cause so much hurt.* Right?

I didn't verbally relay this story to Mr.G after I saw the photograph, but it was clear he already knew…

every detail. There was a tear or two in my eyes. I was incredibly remorseful and completely embarrassed at my lack of compassion concerning a relative stranger whom I now realized was a ***significant*** person in my life. Now I was standing before God...my *sin* exposed.

"I'm so sorry."

Mr.G walked over toward me, put his hand on my shoulder and said, "I know you are."

"Honestly Mr.G, I'm beginning to understand."

Mr.G spoke.

"Now you know how important your earthly journey is. All living things and I don't just mean humanity...all living things are ***significant***. Your relationships are of the utmost importance and the foundation you build for yourself as a human being on earth is what you will build upon for the rest of your existence. Humanity is your family and all the other living things and resources of your planet are yours to protect, love and care for."

"Why don't you just step in and fix the problems of humanity? Our qualities as human beings just don't allow us to always be on our *A-game*. Now I know you could do something about it...just come down and show yourself...people would listen and follow."

"No, they wouldn't...well certainly not everyone. Seriously, there was a time when I attempted to right the ship of your human race. Different methods were incorporated, but I always kept my message of love, compassion, generosity and forgiveness as the constant. It didn't quite work out. I did try again and again, only to finally come to the inevitable conclusion that it was up to humanity to find its own way. I gave you the tools, now it is up to you to make things right…or wrong."

"Sounds like the *prime directive* to me." I spoke.

"*Star Trek*, sure" said Mr.G. "Exactly…I try not to interfere with your culture, so that you can naturally find yourselves. Yes, I believe you've got it!"

"You cannot be serious, Mr.G."

"Oh…but I am." He responded.

"Look at all the evil in the world…the hatred, the pitiful lives so many people have to endure! It doesn't seem equitable that the grim side of life overcomes the goodness so many people have. We just need direction. If you want my opinion, Mr.G, I would do something about it (if I was God), and I wouldn't allow the treachery in the world that goes on day after day and year after year. You have it within you. What is it about *evil* anyway? What is it and why does it exist? Why does it tempt us to do all the bad things we, do?"

"Jim, *evil* truly exists, but it isn't something I can ever explain other than the fact that is just is. There are people in your world that simply embrace pleasure from the misery and hopelessness of others. I do find that repugnant, but in a strange way; *evil* can be a *good thing*."

"How's that?"

Well, when something really terrible happens...take Chuck Taylor of Omaha for example. Many good people lost their life savings because Chucky was greedy and totally ambivalent to the extreme pain he had inflicted. Anyway, Tim Johnson, also of Omaha reached out to some of Chuck's victims and assisted them financially. He asked for nothing in return. Now that was a very *good thing* and it came as a direct result of a sinful deed. So you see, bad things and evil actions can bring out the wonderful goodness (as you said so yourself) that most people have inside their souls. *Evil*, offers *good*, an opportunity to act and those noble endeavors are part of what makes the foundation of your life solid and immovable. This is a *good thing*."

"So is there a hell?" I asked.

"Now that is a tough question...hmmm."

"Actually a yes or a no would suffice, Mr.G."

"In the world you just left, Jim, does your society generally punish criminals by relentlessly torturing them? The answer is, usually no. Obviously prisons aren't pleasant places to live in, but humanity as a whole finds it unacceptable to cause another being, even a criminal, constant agony and pain. So the sentenced felon, now a prisoner is still fed, housed, clothed and given the necessities of life. This is why you are called civilized. Look, I am not a sadistic God. It doesn't make sense for me to have a place where I send people to be eternally punished. You don't do it in your world, why would I do it in mine?"

"So truly evil persons also go to *Heaven*? That wouldn't seem moral or logical."

"On the contrary, truly evil persons by their own actions choose not to exist once they die on Earth."

"And you are their judge? Didn't you say you weren't a judge? Sounds like you are."

"No, Jim, people have free wills and they themselves become their own judge... I simply *facilitate* their sentence." Mr.G said in a somber tone.

We talked for hours as our ship playfully skipped the vast watery pavement. The two suns that gave me so much warmth and pleasure began to sink into the horizon and when that happened; the sky became filled with billions and trillions of stars, galaxies, planets, comets and moons. No fireworks display could every come close to the dazzling presentation of lights and colors I was witnessing...well maybe ...there was one exception.

"Thank you for this gift...God."

Mr.G smiled at me and then simply said...

"You're welcome, James."

It was the very first time I actually addressed this mysterious being with the title of God, and in saying that, I now came to the wondrous conclusion that God did indeed exist. To say the least, it was more than just a momentous occasion for me. There was now affirmation to my existence and also to my spirit, which I now realized would live on for infinity. My lifelong dreams and hopes to really know God finally came to fruition and it certainly was a realization I never thought possible...not in my lifetime...not in a million years. What a kick! How so very cool!

The warm look God gave me at the moment of my *epiphany* was that of a loving Parent, glowing with joy and pure love. Although I felt unworthy of his love, it was obvious he didn't concur with my thoughts.

It's curious how our lives turn out...you just never know from moment to moment. Funny, I always thought my search for the proverbial *Holy Grail*, God, was the ultimate, the end to a long journey, but while I found God for sure, what I perceived as the *prize*, was in error. I was wrong and he was about to show me the way.

"To the world you might be one person, but to one person you might be the world."---Unknown

Family Ties

"Love is a fruit in season at all times and within reach of every hand."
---Mother Teresa

Kao (kay-o) was having the time of her life on this perfectly splendid autumn afternoon, as she swayed from side to side, 50 feet above the forest ground. The sensation of the cool breeze blowing thru her branches tickled, and the glorious sun above, nourished her leaves that numbered in the millions. Kao, now in her 50th year was still very young, especially when it came to white oak trees, and her Mother, just a hundred feet or so away from Kao was almost 150 years old. It was, without question, a magnificent forest where Kao lived...white oak, red oak, spruce, hickories, sugar maple and so many more trees and plants resided there.

Kao loved to play, particularly with the birds that would regularly congregate on her sturdy branches. They loved Kao because she never refused to accommodate them, no matter how many flocked to her. She enjoyed the chirping, whistling and singing that birds are so adept at doing and the melodies they sang lifted her spirits. Life for Kao was simply grand! Being such a large and strong tree allowed Kao to be depended upon by the multitude of animals and insects that made this extraordinary forest their home. Squirrels constructed their nests between Kao's larger branches and hundreds of birds perched on her smaller branches. Her enormous canopy provided protection from the wind and rain, and it kept the animals cool in the summer's heat. The acorns she produced by the ton were an important source of food for the squirrels and other animals that roamed this land. Kao enjoyed her lofty status, but remained ever so humble to those around her. Kao, her Mother and the other fellow trees provided so much to the forest and asked for nothing in return.

"Mother, being a tree is really special...isn't it? Inquired Kao.

"Yes it is Kao...and just to be alive in this blessed land of ours is truly a gift. To never exist would be the cruelest thing, so even if it was for a fleeting moment, I would choose life every time."

Being around for 150 years made Kao's Mother wise, and her years of observation and experience bequeathed to her the knowledge and wisdom that only could come with age.

"Mother, will I someday *not* be a tree? Will I someday *not* exist?"

"Why do you ask me such questions, Kao? Have you been talking with your owl friend again? What is he filling your thoughts with?"

"He told me about a terrible demon he called *fire* that is approaching us at this very moment to destroy us. He said we will be killed! Am I going to die? Are you going to die, Mother?"

"Kao, in the far distance beyond the sugar maples, there is a fire on its way racing toward us. I can assure you it's not a demon, but it is a significant entity concerning the circle of life. The elders have known it for several days, but we chose not to alarm our children this soon. In due time, we were going to talk with you concerning the situation. Now you know, so you have the right to ask questions."

"You told me; the cruelest thing that could happen would be to never exist. Am I *not* going to exist and never be with my friends again...never to be with you, Mother?"

"But Kao, you do exist! Look at you...you're so full of life! I said to *never exist*, but here you are! Please do not be anxious for yourself or for me. Death is merely a change in spirit; it is a new beginning and it is certainly not the end of existence. The spirit within you will transform into new life ... and with it will come the most wonderful forest you could ever imagine. Do you feel my roots beneath the ground hugging you tight, Kao?

"Yes, I do, Mother."

"Then be assured, we are and always will be as one. You and I, as the other trees in this forest are eternally tied to one another...we are forever linked. Death is not a sad circumstance or something to be feared, but death is an incredibly beautiful event that gives our lives and our spirits purpose. Our passing away will bring forth new life and that new life will carry on our legacy as testament to our existence. Kao, have faith in me and in yourself. If you have that kind of strength, you will never be afraid and you will only find peace."

"I think I understand, Mother. I will try not to be afraid."

And so it came to past...in this heavenly woodland... the fire arrived and took Kao and her Mother away. Their ashes were abundant in nutrients... as the other trees that perished in the fire, and this allowed the starving soil to become renewed. The hibernating seeds hidden in the rich and fertile ground were now teeming with life as they mixed with rain and earth. The next spring, thousands of tiny seedlings sprouted toward the life-giving sun and the beginning of a new forest sprung forth. The rebirth began with the red oak, spruce, hickories and sugar maples and yes in the very spots where Kao and her Mother lived were white oaks. They would soon become magnificent trees...*just like their parents.*

> *"Life is to be fortified by many friendships---to love and be loved is the greatest happiness of existence."*
>   *---Sydney Smith*

Exploring

"People like you and I, though mortal of course like everyone else, do not grow old no matter how long we live...(We) never cease to stand like curious children before the great mystery into which we were born."
---Albert Einstein

"A priest, minister and a rabbi walk into a bar. The bartender says...what is this, a joke?"

Mr.G couldn't stop laughing at his quip. It was *cute*, but it wasn't Robin William's material, if you know what I mean. With his *unique* abilities, Mr.G *zapped* us back to the familiar surroundings of the patio at the back of the Italian restaurant. Leaving the schooner was an emotional event for me, because with the absolute realization of God's existence, my thoughts could only focus on more questions about the implications and possibilities of my own *eternal-ness*. Maybe Mr.G could see the wheels turning inside my head and to break up the moment, he hit me with his *best* joke, I suppose.

95

"Maybe you're trying too hard, Mr.G," I spoke.

"Maybe you're being too serious…too philosophical," he said in return.

"I'll admit you're probably right…it's just the turn of events…the car accident, this place…and YOU! I'm overwhelmed and I just don't quite know what to think or what to do."

"You don't have to do anything, Jim…or you can do *something.*"

"What is that supposed to mean?" I inquired with a rather confused look on my face.

"What do you think I mean?"

"Now you're speaking in riddles, Mr.G. Questions can be intriguing, especially coming from you, but at this point in time, *answers* are really what I'm looking for…it would certainly catch my interest. Know what I mean?"

"Interesting, Jim, you have finally come to the affirmation of God's existence and eternal life, yet you continue to yearn for something you're not sure of. It is as if there are still a few missing puzzle pieces in your life. Let me assure you, there are more than just a few pieces unanswered for and the only way to find the answers you seek is to explore and ponder possibilities you may never before have entertained as feasible. In your Earth terms, isn't that thinking *outside the box?*" Ever hear of Ernest H. Shackelton, the Antarctica adventurer? I know you

have. Bet you never thought of yourself as an explorer...
but you are...we all are!"

"I don't know what to say Mr.G. I never really
imagined dying could be so...so complicated. Plenty of
questions...few answers."

"So what's the big deal, Jim? It's not like time is
creeping up on you anymore. You should know that by
now. It should be obvious! Anyway, it is the searching
and the exploration that truly is the most intriguing.
After all, once you have the answer you seek, in most
instances you move on to another question. It's our
nature...it is innate in us. Humanity has a proclivity
for seeking out answers to mysteries. I think that's great!
It is the challenge itself that can be the most rewarding.
What do you think?"

"Yeah, I believe you're right...but..."

"I know Jim, I know. I can sense what troubles you.
You really can be quite transparent. You think maybe
I'm holding back something and that for sure is a definite
possibility. Be patient, ok?"

"So have a little bit of *faith* in you, Mr.G? I'm
beginning to sound like a broken record."

This entire time, God and I were lounging and talking
on the patio. I really couldn't say if a day had passed
or not. When we were on the schooner, we eventually
settled into the evening, star gazing, but here on the patio,

it appeared to be the same beautiful clear day it was when we were *transported* to the ship. The view, the sounds and smells of this absolutely stunning place felt like ice-cold water to the lips of a person gasping with thirst. My senses were continually quenched and even though I still had many unanswered questions, I did enjoy a few moments of peace and solitude.

It took me by surprise as to just how laid-back God was. He did everything he could do to put me at ease, except I kept resisting. Typical me, I thought. Even in death and now eternal life, I was still battling my own demons and insecurities.

"Jimmy, you need to relax…lighten up."

Mr.G walked over to the far end of the patio and reached for a scruffy old-looking brown and yellow broom that was leaning up against the wooden railing. With the broom in his hands, he held it as one would hold a guitar and in an instant the music came out of nowhere and the sound was simply everywhere. The music was a smartly written jazzy electric guitar riff; a song called **Loungin'**… my Chris was the composer. Without any hesitation (or encouragement), Mr.G gyrated and jumped with the funky beat and all of this time I'm just staring in utter disbelief. God thinks he's some kind of *rock star*! Now his joke may have been weak, but his imitation of a guitarist was totally funny and for one of the few times since my *untimely* demise, I just laughed until my stomach hurt. I could have died laughing, but…I was already dead!

"Well God, that certainly was entertaining, but for all of the time you have on your hands, did you ever consider having someone teach you how to play a real guitar? Jimmie Hendrix, maybe? Brooms are ok, but you just can't substitute it for the real thing. It's not the same." I spoke.

"That's what Shackelton tells me, Jim. Explorers envision possibilities, but they also follow thru on their dreams no matter what the risks or consequences…failures or successes. Your son gave up playing brooms a long time ago and he taught himself how to really do it right. He couldn't have done it any other way and I suspect when your youngest finds his niche, he too will go after his dreams full tilt and answer some of his questions. Remember, I said, you don't have do anything or you can do *something*. Jim, finding answers to your unfinished puzzle are out there and you should try a little exploring to discover what you seek. It is after all your conundrum…*not mine*. You can pretend and play the broom your entire life, or you can get true satisfaction by *going for it* with energy and zeal. Funny how a simple tool like an old broom can teach such valuable lessons. You think?"

"You're right, Mr.G, in fact you're not telling me anything I didn't already know. Obviously coming from you pretty much reinforces that notion. It is a difficult thing…*going for it*. When I was alive…well…on Earth… I guess I was too timid or too afraid to be that explorer… always fearing rejection or failure. I always tried to be conservative…too middle-of-the-road…and play it safe. Maybe I screwed up?"

"Now you're being too harsh on yourself, Jim. How many Shackeltons are there in the world? Not many, I can assure you of that…plus every member of humanity has a role whether we want it or not. It really is no big deal… certainly not to me. Is it extra special to see a person use the *max* of his or her talents and skills? Absolutely, but you didn't fumble the handoff, Jim…frankly, your life on Earth was one you should be proud of because for the most part, you lived life with your head on straight and you can't ask for much more than that."

"Thanks for the kind words, Mr.G…it feels good you would think of me in such a manner. I know I was far from perfect…but I did try."

"Who's perfect?" Grinned Mr.G.

"Yeah, who is perfect?" I laughed, remembering my conversation with Mr.G on *his imperfect-ness.*

"You know," continued Mr.G, "The word *perfect* reflects a very positive connotation, yet if you or I were perfect, then what would there be to discover or explore? After all, we would have all of the answers. Where is the fun in that? It would be terribly uninspiring and an incontrovertible bore. Why do you think we have minds to think...and brains to calculate, imagine, decipher and on and on? The answers to most of our queries are out there and it should be our quest to exercise our minds to find the solutions. Can you imagine what it would have been like to be Charles Darwin and come up with the notion of the evolution of living things...or what about Watson and Crick and the discovery of DNA, the very strands of life? And now there is the completion of the human genome, new intriguing theories concerning the creation of your universe! Big Bang! Wow! Discovery, Jim that is where it's happening! It is an astounding part of existence!"

"You said creation, Mr.G? I was taught that you created the universe and all occupants in it, in only 6 days. Granted, I never believed it, but a lot of people still cling to those and other far fetched ideas as to how our universe came about and how human beings evolved...or didn't"

"So now you're some kind of intellectual snob?" retorted Mr.G, "You certainly don't know the answers either...do you?"

"No," I sheepishly replied.

"So if certain religious beliefs explain creation in their own way, why not let them believe it? Remember, I told you that everyone has a role in life. Not every person will grasp or comprehend certain ideas, especially when it comes to how the universe or life was created. I can tell you right now, it doesn't concern me, and frankly if their beliefs help them live lives full of love and compassion, then who am I to deter or shun them. Should I think less of you, Jim, because you're incapable of performing brain surgery or that matrix algebra is just a blur to you? Keep in mind...all of these people are struggling just like you to find their place, their niche, their purpose. All of them are the grains of sand that are so close to you, Jim."

"Significance," I quietly said.

"Yes, *significance."* Spoke Mr.G.

"Jim, if you had your life back on Earth and you decided to *go for it*...what would you do?"

"Well, if I assume that I could retain all of what has happened to me, I would probably attempt to write a book about it. Of course, who would believe me anyway? If I said I saw Elvis or the Loch Ness Monster, then I'd probably have a few believers, but to say I had dinner and conversation with the Creator himself and then came back from the grave to tell all about it...well...I'd be laughed out of town."

"So, do you care...you know...that no one would believe you?" Inquired Mr.G.

"Yes," I said emphatically.

"Really, Jim, why should it matter? I think you should do it with all the passion and drive you can muster. Mostly do it for yourself…after all you've always wanted to write. Think of it as therapy for your soul. That is what *going for it* is all about…never to be afraid of what others might think, because what other people's opinions may be…well…when it comes to the end of the day…that's all they are…opinions."

"Uh, in case your memory has gone amiss, Mr.G, I believe it is a little bit too late for that now. I suppose, I too became one of those *lemmings.*"

"Maybe, but truthfully it isn't a crime and frankly, we're all lemmings at one time or another." Spoke Mr.G.

There was an awkward silence between the two of us for what seemed about a half hour or so, as we drifted off in our thoughts. I couldn't help being overwhelmed by feelings of regrets, lost opportunities and dumb mistakes I made in my life. I understood what God had told me about my life being a very decent and admirable one…but that was his view…my mind was telling me otherwise. Funny, I finally made it to eternity and discovered God, but I still found myself more unsettled than ever.

"Mr.G, I always tried to imagine what it would be like to meet you face to face…that is…if you even existed. This is not quite what I had pictured."

"You sound disappointed," Spoke Mr.G.

"No, on the contrary, not disappointed at all. I did think if I ever made it to eternal life though...things would be less complicated...no...as a matter of fact... not complicated at all! But seeing you here?...not a disappointment at all. Meeting your acquaintance has been a revelation and that is a *good thing.*"

"You can never possibly know all or even most of the answers, Jim. While dying and going to *Heaven* is remarkable, it may not solve the mysteries and secrets of life you are seeking. It will though, reveal the most critical answer you crave...you just don't know the question yet and I suspect you will eventually solve the answer without knowing the question first. In fact people on Earth at this very moment, don't even need to visit *Heaven* to find this out. It's pretty much of a no-brainer."

"You said you might be holding back and it's clear you won't tell me anything without me discovering it for myself. After all, I am the explorer...correct?"

"You've got that right, Jim."

"Are you Jesus Christ?" I blurted out.

Oh boy...I'm telling myself. Where did that come from...leftfield? This was a question that had been on my mind for quite some time, but the one I was afraid to ask. What was I thinking? I guess I wanted to wait for the right time...if there ever was a right time. Instead of thinking it thru, I just asked. Talk about *going for it!*

"What do you think, Jim?"

"I really don't know Mr.G. Maybe it doesn't really matter…maybe I shouldn't have asked the question. You are God and you did say most religions have it right…in principal anyway. You know…it was just inappropriate to ask. I'm sorry."

"What's to be apologetic about? It's a perfectly reasonable question, but as you might suspect, the answer isn't totally apparent. How can I answer you? Hmmmmm…in order for humanity to know of me and understand my existence, do you think I would appear or show myself to just a small select group of individuals. Do you think I would only choose people of Christian beliefs, or Judaism, or Islam etc. etc.? What about the inhabitants of the rain forests of the Amazon, or prehistoric man living in North America, or any group of human beings in any time or place for that matter? There are many ways to bring messages to believers in God and well let's just say I have experimented with a variety of *methods*. I guess you could say I'm kind of like a *gardener.*"

"A gardener?" I asked.

"Yes. Traveling around the world, it is plain to see that geographically, the Earth can vary quite a bit. There are different climates and soil conditions that lend themselves to growing specific types of plants and trees. For example; I can grow oranges in Florida, but I can't do that in Siberia. The chemical make-up of soil on the Plaines of Iowa is quite different than the soils of Australia. So you can see; what I can grow in one place may not work for another. I have planted seeds all over the Earth, and the life that comes from those seeds is dependent on the time and conditions it came from. Someday soon, you will come to understand what I am telling you and in knowing this wisdom, you will then know… *who I am.*"

"Hmmm…a gardener. What's *Heaven* like? Hell… um…I mean heck…I might as well get all of these questions out of my system."

"Do you remember the one episode in the sitcom *Seinfeld,* where Neumann, Kramer and I believe George are in a car and they are discussing the days of the week?"

"Yeah, it was funny. Monday had a *feel,* Tuesday didn't…I think…"

"Right," interrupted Mr.G. "Well *Heaven* also has a *feel*…actually many *feels*."

At that moment, everything around me went pitch black. I was no longer sitting, lying down, standing or anything. I guess you could say I was floating, because that is the only way I could describe the sensation and although I was surrounded in total darkness, I could see my body perfectly and it seemed to be illuminated by a dull glow. It was ...very cool! The complete quiet and stillness around me was like no other silence I had ever experienced and the tranquility was inexplicable. How strange...I was thinking...how peculiar. Where was I? Is this *Heaven...* and where...is God?

In the infinite distance of the space I was now occupying, I could see a tiny speck of light. Was it a star, a moon, a galaxy? I certainly couldn't tell, (and I probably wouldn't know anyway), and since it was the only visible thing, with the exception of myself, I stayed focused on it.

You know, being around God, it was evident, most of his actions and conversations with me concluded by having some kind of meaning or lesson. He chose to challenge me with his questions and was always intensely inquisitive concerning my answers and reactions. I think he was the original *Curious George*. If I was an explorer as he suggested, then God was the ultimate explorer, ever probing and penetrating the universe. I had now come to realize, the loneliness I had sensed in him was not that, as much as it was his uncertainty of his own identity. Eventually most of humanity will come to terms with their mortal lives by simply jumping head first into eternity and then meeting their Creator, but for God, it was another matter...especially when the subject matter pertained to his own creation. He *just didn't know,* it was that simple…and although humanity was a product of his creativity, I am convinced, it was us…human beings…he sensed could bring him closer to his own humanity…his self…his being.

This by far was the ultimate drug. Here I was floating, and the euphoria completely enveloped my entire body and soul with feelings I was certainly never aware of. I could touch my fingers and see with clarity as the interaction of nerve cells transferred the signal to my brain that immediately sent a warm and exhilarating sensation thru-out my body. These *exquisite vibes* were rapidly firing at me…non-stop, and with each passing second, a different and even more pleasurable *feel* would arrive. All at once, a low humming or buzzing sound reached my ears and it would seem it was coming from the incomprehensible speck of light…it was. If the *4th of July* or a *Pink Floyd* concert were anything like this, then there wouldn't be anybody wanting to do anything else but be here. This tiny dot of light became an instant explosion that *blacked out* the darkness with intense lights and colors that this writer could never have imagined or conceived of. Absolutely every atom in my body was being drenched with gushing happiness, delirious joy and oh boy…the *hits just kept coming*! I wasn't about to tell anyone to stop this ride. All I can be sure of is *Heaven* has *billions and billions* of *feels* and you want every one of them! Talk about instant addiction! I guess asking God...*what Heaven was like,* was an excellent choice for a question. Know what I mean?

The expression *all good things must end* or something like that doesn't really pertain to *Heaven*...I think, but for me...my *coming attractions tour* was finished and in an instant, I wasn't where I was, but found myself standing alongside a crystal clear pond in the middle of a quiescent and remote meadow. There was a soft breeze pushing and tugging on the slender reeds and whistling thru the surrounding oak, maple and evergreen trees. This tiny body of water seemed so serene and placid, yet the flourish of activity below the surface was what could only be described as a frenzy of movement. I could see the different schools of fish dashing and darting at sharp angles...always instinctively moving with the group and the turtles kept snapping up at the surface as mosquitoes and other delectable insects took their chances as they hit the water. There were petite and colossal boulders protruding from the pond and it was on one of the largest boulders I stood...watching several frogs leap from here to there ever so effortlessly. Looking away from the pond, the meadow stretched on forever in every direction. It was without doubt a wonderful and beautiful place to be in. I was first thinking to myself that I was alone, but then I could see on the horizon…two figures walking toward me on a long winding narrow dirt path. They were too far in the distance for me to identify them, but it wouldn't be long until we would be face to face.

It was rather compelling and even though my curiosity was now peaking; there was one overwhelming question on my mind. Where was God?

"Success is to be measured not so much by the position that one has reached in life as by the obstacles which he has overcome while trying to succeed."
---Booker T. Washington

Harry and Bottle

"Don't be afraid of the space between your dreams and reality. If you can dream it, you can make it so."
---Belva Davis

If I knew by asking God, *"What's Heaven like?"* and that he would just *disappear* into thin air, I'm sure I wouldn't have asked the question. Frankly, I missed the guy and I was afraid that our *meeting* was finished. The *ride*, as I have come to call it, was truly beyond my wildest expectations, but I would have given it up to be with God again, even if for only a moment. I desperately wanted to thank him for everything and more. No doubt, there was now a bond present between the two of us and I finally was beginning to understand my relationship with him. This was a *good thing*. To me, he was a Father, teacher and eventually a friend…no a *best* friend. He asked nothing from me and yet he was clearly willing and eager to give and spend eternity with me. Now, he was nowhere in sight.

In the distance, I could distinctly tell, the two figures coming toward me on the dirt path were a man and a woman. They appeared elderly, yet their gait was not of the *geriatric set* but of much younger persons, moving briskly and with a playful purpose. Their faces?…I couldn't quite make them out…yet. It seemed apparent they were enamored with each other, because for most of the time I observed, they were holding hands as if they were boyfriend and girlfriend or husband and wife. The woman seemed energetically *frisky* as she would skip, hop and dance from one side of the path to the other, picking bouquets of colorful flowers and sticking them in the nose of her partner. These two *senior citizens* were having a grand time, giggling and laughing as they merrily headed my way. The man at one point even flung himself headfirst toward the ground, only to catch the earth with his strong hands and then amazingly started walking on them. Needless to say, this was a most curious sight!

They were now within a short distance of maybe 50 yards and my heart stopped cold, and my face felt flush. Just ahead of me were two persons I knew oh so well. It seemed like a million years ago since I last saw or spoke to my Mother's parents…my Grandparents; Michael and Clara, aka *Harry and Bottle*.

Grandpa was undeniably great and always so full of life and combustible energy. He had a terrifically kind heart that he shared unselfishly with his family and friends. I remember how he used to play all sorts of games with me and my brothers and sister. He would teach us games like jarts, bumper pool, and oh yeah, he loved to play croquet in his backyard. He had a uniquely funny way of taking the wooden mallet and then looking down between his legs to make his shot. What I remember most about him was that he was a compassionate caring man and the *skinny* of it all is that he was simply a quality human being. Apparently God thought so too, after all, Grandpa was now standing directly in front of me.

My Grandmother, Clara was affectionately given the nickname *Bottle* by my Grandfather because of her affinity for collecting all sorts of glass bottles. While Harry was gregarious, Bottle was quiet and reserved, always saving her wise words and kind actions when needed and never ever complaining or saying an unkind thought concerning anyone. We were tireless children as I recall and when we paid Grandma and Grandpa a visit…well…I don't know how Grandma stayed so calm, collected and tolerant with us. My Mother said she had the *patience of Jobe* and my observations of my Grandmother over the years confirmed that notion. She was the ultimate best and apparently God thought so too, after all Grandma was now standing directly in front of me.

When I was 35, Grandpa passed away due to a sudden heart attack. Up to that point in my life, I had never really known anyone as well as I knew him that had died. Nine years later, Grandma's courageous fight with diabetes came to an end.

The phrase *distance makes the heart grow fonder,* was something I never bought into. *Out of sight, out of mind,* seemed to be my motto and unfortunately with the passing of time, I though less and less of my Grandparents. Now with them standing before me, my buried feelings of love for them simply overpowered me. Like a bolt of lightning, it struck me just how much I had really missed them and how I yearned to see them and hear their voices again.

I suppose we are often times convinced that we have plenty of time at our disposal…time to visit a friend or relative…time to forgive…time to say *I'm sorry*…time to show compassion and generosity or time to exhibit and express our love for someone. We don't. On Earth, the moments we experience and share are finite. These miniscule events in time offer us (humanity), ever so brief windows of opportunity to act and do the right thing. We can be stubborn, lazy or selfish by ignoring and squandering our chances or we can accept the challenges and embrace the human relationship to its fullest.

Tears of joy quietly fell to the ground and as each drop softly kissed the soil, beautifully colored flowers burst forth at my feet, each one tickling and caressing my toes. Ha! I wasn't even aware that I didn't have any shoes on!

For several minutes we had not spoken a single word to each other, but eventually they reached for me, opened their arms and embraced me. Oh how it felt! Oh God... it felt like...like *Heaven*!

"Grandpa! Grandma! I can't believe this...it's you! I'm flabbergasted...stunned! I do love you both!"

"Jimmy! We know how you feel and we love you too!" Spoke Grandma.

"It's so great to see you and be with you again!" Added Grandpa.

Strange...at that moment my feet felt heavy...no actually more like something coming from the ground and grabbing at my ankles and keeping me from moving.

"I can't seem to move...I don't know why" I spoke.

"Don't you understand?" Inquired Grandma. "It's us! The roots that tie us together are forever and eternal. That is what you feel. We are one, just as we've always been. Dying on Earth never destroyed the bond...the love. Love never weakens...it only gets stronger."

We talked for what seemed hours. It was like old times and I just couldn't get enough of them. We discussed all sorts of things; about my life, my children, MJ and they especially wanted to talk about their children and how much they longed to be with them again. Even in *Heaven,* I now could see, without their children, there was still a piece missing in their spirit and they were eager to fill that void.

"I guess you didn't figure I'd get here before them... did you?"

"You had to follow your own path to arrive here, Jim. Some paths are shorter than others." Spoke Grandpa.

"We miss Marilyn and Joe (my parents) as we do our boys and their families, but we know they will come here when their paths run out...you know...when they're ready." Said Grandma.

"I wasn't ready, Grandma! I didn't want to leave, but here I am! Look, I was relatively young and I still had so much to do. I know you can die at any age, but I really thought I'd grow old with MJ and maybe enjoy my boys as adults. This isn't the worst thing that could have happened to me, but I wasn't expecting this anyway! I was caught off-guard! Know what I mean?"

"I've got a feeling, Mr.G might have special plans for you," Spoke Grandpa. "You've been here for quite some time and it usually doesn't work that way."

"So if I understand you correctly, once you die, generally you get a straight shot to *Heaven*? You're suggesting, when I died...I somehow hit a detour...a Mr.G *pit stop*? Unbelievable!"

"That sounds about right." Replied Grandpa.

"You said, Mr.G...does everyone call him that?"

"No, said Grandpa, but I've been giving him bowling lessons and he told me he preferred Mr.G...He calls me Harry."

"Bowling? Huh...how's he doing?" I asked.

"Between you me? Not too well. Poor foot work and no hook to his ball. I am determined to make him better though and of course I've got plenty of time to accomplish that."

The three of us talked for a bit more, but it was obvious to me, our visit was coming to an end. I didn't want it to end. Harry motioned to Bottle with a gentle elbow to her ribs. It was time for them to leave.

"Where are you going? Can I come with you?"

I acted like a pathetic little puppy dog...my ears perked up, my nose sweaty and my tail anxiously wagging from side to side.

"We're going home, but it's not time for you...not yet anyway." Spoke Grandpa.

"Why not? I'm dead too you know! Please! I'm lost...I'm lonesome."

"Jimmy," replied Grandpa, "Believe me, you're going to be all right and we will eventually meet up with you again, and when that *again* occurs, you can come home with us. I promise."

"So have a little bit of *faith* in you too? Maybe you're talking too much with Mr.G!" I said.

Grandma looked at me with a smile.

"Yes, have faith in yourself first and in those who love you. That should pretty much *wrap it up.* It's that simple, Jim…trust us. Tell our children we love them and we will be together soon…as one…as it should be. We love you too…you know that already…so good-bye for now."

It was that abrupt…believe me! I did a frantic 360, but my Grandparents were nowhere to be seen. My head dropped to my chest, as I now fully understood…I was alone again. Why was Grandma telling me to say hello to her children anyway? I think once you get to *Heaven*, you learn to specialize in ambiguous statements and riddles.

I looked around just once more, hoping to see someone, but instead, what I saw was terribly disturbing and even frightening. I hadn't noticed it coming, but the weather changed dramatically. There was a frigid breeze racing across the cloud covered meadow and the normally active pond was void of any real movement except for the sharp ripples of water that were being pushed and whipped by a piercing and unforgiving wind. A chilly…

misty rain was beginning to fall, while the green leaves that dressed the surrounding trees, were instantly turning brown and were being forcefully snapped, plucked and blown away far off into the distance. I was uncomfortably cold, probably because I had no shoes and my only real protection from the elements were my blue jeans and sweatshirt. There was a park bench along the water's edge of the pond in the meadow, so I sat there and curled up my legs to keep warm. I was sadly and completely alone...no family, no friends, no Grandparents...and no Mr.G. As I sat, there was a quick burst of wind that whistled past my left ear and onto the bench, next to me, dropped an old ragged newspaper. Huh? The newspaper headline caught my attention.

"Husband... Father, killed in Spectacular Crash"

A funny and not-so-funny accident happened to me when I was probably in my early 30's. MJ and I were doing some yard work one humid summer day and we went into the garage to retrieve some garden utensils. I didn't notice the metal tooth rake lying face up on the garage floor and needless to say, I stepped on the upright end of the rake, causing the wooden handle to fly straight up, hitting me with great force, square on my forehead. It's true! Believe me...you literally do see stars! Except for a large knot on my forehead and a bruised ego, (MJ saw the whole thing), I was ok.

Looking at the words on the newspaper headline... **Husband...Father**, struck me harder than that rake handle ever could. God was right...I found the answer before I ever knew the question!

What made me the happiest and most fulfilled when I was alive, was my wife and children. They were the crucial pieces of my puzzle that absolutely completed my life and soul. When I was on Earth, I couldn't solve the problems of the world or understand why humanity was always in constant turmoil and my search for God was in vain…but God must have thought well of MJ and the boys, because they were always there, standing directly in front of me…all I really had to do was open my eyes! It was my family that truly made me whole and they were always the best reason in the world to be alive! I always thought the *question* was *what in my life can make me the happiest?* Now it was clear to me, it was *who…who in my exploration of the universe can fill my needs, complete my life and love me for myself?*

I sat on the bench and silently cried. There was a wondrous gratification that I had come to know the truth, but there was a tremendous sadness and loneliness that bathed itself upon my shaking body. I called out to God, asking him to give me back my earthly life. I wanted to be with my family once again and I wanted a second chance to be a better human being to those who were significant to me.

The leaves whisked by me as if they were in a race with each other and the howling wind whispered a sad refrain of lost chances and missed opportunities. All of a sudden, I felt a warm comforting hand resting on my shoulder and without turning around, I knew it was *him*.

"Where were you?" I asked.

"Bowling," he said.

"Bowling? Huh. Rumor has it…you bowl as well as you take slap shots."

"Really? You've been talking to Harry?"

"Have you been doing anything else besides bowling, Mr.G? You have been gone for quite some time."

"Oh you know, a little bit of *dis* and a little bit of *dat*, said a joking Mr.G in his rather poor imitation of a *wise guy*. Did you think I left you?"

"No, I said…well maybe."

"Sorry, I'm kind of a busy guy…you know…being God, the Creator and all of that."

"That's ok," I said.

"No, Jim…this is ok!"

Just like that…BAM! (Where's *Emeril* when you need him?!)…we're back at the ice arena. Mr.G smiled at me with a sneaky kind of grin and spoke.

"Jim…speaking of rumors…it has come to my attention that you might wish to go back…back to your family?"

He peered directly at me and all I could do was look back at him.

"Facts do not cease to exist because they are ignored."
---Aldous Leonard Huxley

A Puzzling Situation

"When our eyes see our hands doing the work of our hearts, the circle of creation is completed inside us, the doors of our souls open, and love steps forth to heal everything in sight."
---Michael Bridge

Love is an enigma. You can't touch, see, smell or hear it, yet few of us would disagree that love does not exist. It does. Love has an unquestionable presence.

It wasn't all that long ago, I was viewing a television program on the *tangible-ness* of love. Some astute researchers and scientists had been able to measure particular chemical activity and brain wave patterns in individuals they felt could ascertain what the *love* emotion was. It was suggested, what human beings feel in the *love experience* is a complex combination of physiological components, bioelectric entities and chemical neurotransmitters doing their thing. While I don't pretend to even be an amateur concerning this form of academic study, this information, as I understood it, certainly sounded plausible. We are after all human beings and human beings are biological creatures that are *put together* with all sorts of goodies that make us who we are. This is real science, but there are some things the human body is comprised of that simply cannot be measured and if one stretched his imagination a bit, the idea of love can take on a new meaning in our lives.

Enter your newborn's nursery in the middle of the night and softly lay your hand on that sleeping child. You can immediately sense a wonderful feeling that becomes uniquely yours. The tenderness, the quiet and the warmth you experience is *love.* So you can touch love…love has a *feel.* Look into the eyes of your Mother or Father, Parents that maybe have been there for you your entire life, in good and unpleasant times. See how they look at you? You can *see* love. Your child is laughing or crying, or maybe you are listening to your Grandparents conversing with you or giving you advise you so desperately seek. Clearly, love *can be heard.* Now breathe in the air around your significant other…the fragrance of their hair or the scent of their skin will trigger sensations of closeness, bonding and a comfortable familiarity. It is now easy to understand the implication…loves even possesses a *smell.* Interesting…wondrously mind-boggling…I think so. Love is a very *good thing.*

Mr.G and I were back in the relaxed atmosphere of the *JLA*. We weren't near the ice rink though, but in a section of the complex I could only describe as a cafeteria. It was a spacious room with at least 20 large tables, all in different styles and colors and a wide assortment of chairs that were scattered about. Some tables would have 2 chairs, some 4…needless to say it was what I might call *mish-mash*. On each table there was a white linen tablecloth that hinted to be hiding something and I say that only because in the middle of each table, the cloth covering would slightly bulge up. There was one exception.

On the table next to where I was standing, was a large, uncovered and incomplete jigsaw puzzle and to my amazement, the puzzle was a photograph of me. Should I have been surprised? Knowing Mr.G much better now, I would have to say *no*…not at all!

"What gives, Mr.G?"

"I thought you might like to see this place. It may be a somewhat crude or even rudimentary way of keeping track of people's lives, but I find it quite intriguing and exceptional. Everyday these puzzles change as the lives of humanity roll on and on. It's a considerable inspiration seeing pieces of lives discovered and explored and to watch the growth and progress taking place. I realize these linens are concealing up the others at this moment, but it's a privacy thing, you know."

"So this partially finished jigsaw puzzle of myself, in essence is my life? I asked.

"Yeah, interesting…huh?"

"Ha! It figures. Loot at *all* the missing spaces! You would think by just dying alone, maybe there would be only a few pieces left…*God forbid*… maybe even a complete picture…no…not me!"

"I told you Jim, there will always be searching, exploring and discovery and it certainly goes beyond dying on Earth. Why don't you take the two pieces you have in your hand and fit them in the puzzle?"

"What? Where did these come from?" I spoke while opening my hand, only to find two pieces as Mr.G said.

"It's your life, how should I know? Responded Mr.G.

Not surprisingly, one of the pieces was in the shape of a heart and on the backside of it was a photo of MJ and the boys. The piece also fit exactly in the area where my heart was. It wasn't tough to decipher its meaning. On the backside of the second piece, was a photo of Mr.G wearing his hockey gear. He even autographed it! That piece precisely fit where my forehead was. I guess I could understand that too. My love for my family was rekindled and my search for God truly had come to an end.

"You know Jim, surprisingly you haven't said much about your family, yet the heart-shaped puzzle piece clearly shows, without any doubt, they are and always will be the most significant to you."

"That is why it shouldn't confound you Mr.G. From the moment I came to terms with my death, an aching hole in my spirit wouldn't go away. I realized I couldn't be with them for a long time and I wished I could have said good-bye and told them just one last time how much love I had inside of me. I do love them now...more than ever! I suppose by not talking about them was my way of compensating for my loss. Look, Mr.G, when you're ice skating at full speed and slapping pucks around the way you do, I can tell it's your way of distracting yourself, even if it is only temporary...to forget the worries and fears that you might have. You may be God, but you're very human too."

"Ha, so now you're my mentor...my teacher?"

"That's what humanity is all about. We live, grow and learn together. While we teach our children, we also learn from them and it's this process that makes it all worthwhile. I terribly miss my family and friends, but I am glad they are a part of me...even now...as I am a part of them. This wretched loneliness I feel without them is still worth it to me, because the warmth of their love overcomes everything, a thousand times over and more. It was wonderful to be alive and to you God, I am thankful."

"Jim, come out to the rink with me…let's talk some more."

"All truths are easy to understand once they are discovered;
the point is to discover them."
---Galileo Galilei

Parachute

"I can't do what ten people tell me to do, so I guess I'll remain the same…" ---Otis Redding/Steve Cropper…from the song Sitting on the Dock of the Bay

Why are some of the simplest concepts so complicated? Why does humanity fight off what they know to be true, thereby increasing the degree of difficulty in their lives? Too often, we embrace lies and discard truth as if it's a perfectly normal function of our being. Why? Till the day we die and beyond, human beings to some degree will always be in discord with the *law of opposites*, or *you can't have one without the other* law. For example, I would agree, in order to experience happiness, one would have to know what it feels like to be sad and vice versa. This is something most of us know. Human emotions seem to require a reference of comparison in order for them to exist, and if this is true, the feeling of love needs hate and the idea of good needs evil. There is no science I'm aware of to explain this phenomenon and even Mr.G couldn't give me a reasonable explanation. Simply put, this would appear the way of the universe and how it works.

What I had come to understand from Mr.G were ideas that I had already been aware of. They were always right there in front of me, yet the typical human being I am, I chose to complicate even the simplest concepts. From our conversations there were particular thoughts Mr.G emphasized when it came to the simple rules of life.

Understand, we are destined to make many mistakes and the key is not to dwell in the failure, but to learn and grow from those errors.

There will be moments of despair, depression and tragedy and it is imperative to realize this is part of what human existence is about. It is up to us (humanity) to push thru the pain and move on.

Most things bestowed to us on Earth are gifts and should be treated as such. There is significance to these offerings and to ignore or discard this generosity is truly a serious blunder.

Continue to explore and ask questions concerning the universe and embrace science as a tool to discover the answers.

Learn the practice of tolerance and understanding when it comes to the religious or non-religious beliefs of others.

Always be truthful to yourself and others.

Be generous to those who are without.

Show compassion to those who hurt and kindness to those who are alone and lonely.

Avoid vengeance and embrace forgiveness.

Never hesitate to express or show love.

Mr.G and I returned to the place where this unusual adventure of ours began. The arena was dark and the only lights on were directly above the ice rink. We were standing alongside the icy pond, listening to the pleasant silence.

"Did you think I was holding you captive?" Asked Mr.G.

"No, but my Grandfather mentioned I was here maybe longer than usual. Was he right?" I inquired.

"Well, Jim, you have been here admittedly a tad longer than I anticipated, but I was enjoying your visit so much, I didn't think you would mind. Besides, you've always had a choice to stay home *here* or go back home *there*. I thought you figured that out by now."

"Home, there? You mean like Earth home, back with MJ, Chris and Andrew?"

"Of course Earth home, unless you preferred Mars... it can be arranged you know."

"No, no, Earth would be just fine." I said.

"Jim, look at the very top of the arena and tell me what you see."

"The two doors with the brass handles and the illuminated steps. I know *Heaven* is beyond those doors... we've discussed that, Mr.G"

"Yes, but do you recall how you mentioned a certain

curiosity concerning the brass handles?"

"Yeah, they're not always there. They weren't there when Diego went thru...but any other time I've looked up, the handles were present."

"Exactly right," said Mr.G. "You see, for Diego, it was most definitely his time to be here, so he didn't require any handles on the doors because they were going to open up for him anyways. You saw that...but Jim, from the time you arrived here, you have always had a choice...I just didn't tell you that. You can walk up those steps, grab the brass handles, open the doors and enter.

Sha-zam! You've made it! You are in *Heaven*! On the other hand, you can also choose not to open the doors and...well...I would have no other option but to send you back...Earth-bound."

"Wow!..."

"Yeah, pretty cool, huh?" asked Mr.G.

"Very cool!" I said as he threw his hand toward my direction giving me a high-five.

"Remember Jim, if you decide to return to Earth... there is no turning back. I can only do this once. You have felt how wonderful *Heaven* can be and you know life on Earth can be difficult. You sure you want this?"

"Trust me, Mr.G, I know what I want and what I need right now is my family."

"So you're asking me to have a little *faith* in you?"

"Ha, ha, yeah Mr.G, do you think you can handle that?"

"You bet."

At that moment, I found myself standing with my back toward the edge of a cliff and looking down over my shoulder, I peered into the abyss. It seemed to have no bottom in sight and I instantly felt dizzy. I guess I did a few right things in my life, because God was standing directly in front of me. He smiled and reached for my arm to steady myself.

"So, Jim, do you think you can handle this?"

"Is this your idea of a joke, Mr.G? Pretty frightening, don't you think?"

"I just wanted to confirm your resolve in returning to your family. You do know, this is the only way back to Earth," Mr.G spoke while pointing his finger downward beyond the cliff.

"So where is my parachute? Please God, don't say it isn't necessary."

"It isn't necessary, Jim."

"So I guess this is it, huh Mr.G?"

"No, it's just your beginning. Now you have a few more thoughts to contemplate and meditate in the early morning hours when you can't sleep. You know, it's much easier to just stay here, but leaving is not a bad thing at all. You need more time and you really haven't reached the end of your earthly path. If you want to know a secret, Jim, I have always listened to you when you talked to me, even when you were a small child. Surprised? Let's just say that *your ways are not my ways.* Sound familiar?"

I felt embarrassed and ashamed for all those years of doubt, but the goodness of God showed me that he understood. How was I to know? Faith? I suppose, but faith isn't necessarily that easy to come by and besides, God told me I needed to prioritize my life by securing solid relationships and foundations with other human beings...first and foremost. ***Significance.*** Like he said, *Heaven* is timeless and isn't going anywhere, but the human condition on Earth is finite and needs to be attended to *stat.* That's about as simple as it gets.

"I'm sorry, but I just couldn't see you. But that's in the past Mr.G and like you said, it's just the beginning. I'm not naïve to think going home will be easy, but I can assure you, my mind and heart will always be at peace knowing you...God, will be listening to me at night when I need to talk. I hope you too will find the answers you seek, so that you can define your own existence and have comfort in your spirit. Thank you God, for everything."

He smiled at me and in one fluid motion; he reached out to me with his left hand and gently nudged me on my chest. I went from zero to instant super velocity. We've all heard when you die, your entire life flashes in front of you, and while that may be the case for some, it didn't happen to me when I was in my automobile accident. On the other hand, the reverse run from death back to life...I can tell you it did happen! Here I was ripping and speeding toward Earth and my life's history from dying to crying as an infant was right there, figuratively standing in front of me. I suppose it was Mr.G's way of showing me exactly why I decided to go back. For all the pain, sorrow, tragedy and uncertainty there is in life, the enigmatic emotion of love overwhelms everything and makes it all worthwhile.

Quite unexpectedly, the maddening race for *terra firma* stopped and I quietly and gently started to fall in a soft slow-motion. My eyes were now closed and all I could think of were the two words...*welcome home*!

"Good morning Jim...time to get up."

What a wonderful sound. It was my MJ. I got up and reached out my hands for hers. I pulled her toward me and just hugged her for what seemed like forever. It felt...well it felt like *Heaven*!

The *heavenly* feeling was abruptly broken up by the loud crashing sound of my front living room window. There was shattered glass everywhere and as I looked on the floor, I spotted a black rubber disc lying next to the couch. It was a hockey puck! The doorbell rang and I walked toward the door and opened it. Standing right in front of me was a tall man, holding a hockey stick and wearing a *Detroit Red Wing* jersey. How strange!

"Hi, I'm your new neighbor down the block. I was out here in the street, attempting to teach my two sons how to take a slap shot and well, as you can see, I need the practice myself. I'm really sorry…let me help you clean up this mess I've created for you. I'll certainly pay for the damages."

"No, don't worry about it," I said, "besides, it's just a window…there are more important things in life to be concerned with…know what I mean? By the way, my name is Jim and this is my wife Mary Jane."

"You'll have to excuse my poor manners (and poor shooting). My name is Gary…**G**ary **O'D**onnell. Even under these circumstances, it's a pleasure to meet your acquaintance."

"Don't think anything of it…it's nice to meet you too." I said.

"I'd still like to repay you in some way. You know…I own a small nursery in town and if you ever were in need of new plants, shrubs or maybe even a tree…it's on me. I'm a master gardener."

I smiled and just said, "I know."

"Shower the people you love with love. Show them the way that you feel. Things are gonna be much better if you only will." ---James Taylor singer/writer

Lost and Found

"A journey of a thousand miles begins with a single step."
---Confucius

A continuous and determined search for God, ourselves, or our *purpose* on Earth is indeed a noble endeavor and whether we are cognizant of that fact or not, there isn't a member of humanity that doesn't share the same quest. In the end, all of our paths, as diverse as they may be, lead to one common road and it is on this road… the realization of just how special and unique we are, comes to fruition. In some instances, like mine, it was God who found me. Go figure! There is a biblical story about the Shepard and his lost sheep, and I suppose that is how I sometimes saw myself…lost and alone… with no rudder to steer my life and no evening star in the night to point me the way home. For me, God is that Shepard…he is the guiding light…and it is obvious to me; he has plans for each and every one of us. That is the best comfort of all. He wants us to build our eternal foundation here… today, tomorrow and on and on until we take our last breath on Earth. He's right, you know. I can now see his love in all the people that have always meant the most to me. They are my *significant* others.

Love, after all, is a very *good thing* and it is love in the end that will take us to the very *doorsteps of Heaven*.

"Love and family is like peanut butter and jelly…somehow they're just destined for each other."
---*j.j. Giordano*

The End

Epilogue...Love Letters

Ultimately in the end, each individual person who has ever walked this Earth will have to come to terms with his mortality. Our precious lives are finite...and this can only mean the time clock of our lives is ticking... ticking. Maybe we should react to this notion by acting now before we become *lemmings* and run past the real importance of our existence.

There are many *significant* people in our lives...more than we could ever imagine...and a declaration of caring, friendship or love in the form of a letter or poem is a terrific and beautiful way to let someone know how wonderful they are. How many times do we just want to tell someone how special they are...but don't? Lost opportunities...swallowed into the *black hole* of time. Mr.G in this story of mine sees us as tiny grains of sand, all as significant as the other, and all inter-related to each other.

So in conclusion, I think we should get out our pens and paper or power on our word processors...and write to persons in our lives that we care so much about. There really are no permanent things on this Earth...except kindness, respect, compassion, and love. It is up to us (humanity) to somehow go beyond our petty dislikes, fears and even hatred, so that our *fast and furious* lives can truly find peace.

My Dearest Mary Jane,

It is not as if you didn't have many choices…
I'm sure you did.
But some crazy notion of yours, told you…that
I might be the one!

It has been many years since I first laid eyes on you
And now…today…you are still mine!
How can that be?
Why have I been so fortunate…so blessed?

With you I can do so much…
Even when I think I can't…because…
You know I can.

You are my confidant…my lover…
My best friend!

If I were an eagle
I would always soar above you…
Protecting you from harm.

If I were a kangaroo
I'd let you snuggle in my pouch…
To keep you warm.

If I were a lioness and you were my cub
I'd softly and gently nuzzle you with my nose…
To let you know…I am there for you.

If we were elephants
We would take long lazy walks…
With your trunk wrapped around my tail.

We could sit in the sun
Absorbing its precious warmth…
If we were turtles.

Let's be a pair of squirrels…
So I can chase you…
Up and down that maple tree of ours!
Or maybe…
We could just make ourselves a soft cushy nest
Between the sturdy branches…
If we were robins.

I want to be your puppy dog
So I can curl up…
On your lap.

If I were a gardener…
You would be my sunflower

If I were "Dis"
You would be "Dat"!

I swear I can live without my heart... but...
I cannot live if...
I cannot have your love.

I'm sorry for any hurt I may have caused you
I ask for your forgiveness.
My only wish in this last half of my life...
Is to be with you and simply love you... forever.

You have always been "enough" for me...
Enough to fill my soul and spirit...
With feelings so wonderful and inexplicably grand!

Thank you... Mary Jane Louise... for loving this old guy....
Jim

On the doorsteps of Heaven...

2006

Amée

James J. Giordano was born in Detroit, Michigan on a cold blustery February in 1953, and continues to live in Michigan with his wife Mary Jane and two boys, Christopher and Andrew. Jim graduated from Ferris State College in 1977 with a bachelor's degree in Pharmacy and since 1977 he has been a practicing registered Pharmacist. Jim is an avid sports fan (go Wings, Pistons, Tigers and U of M Wolverines!!), and he also enjoys reading and writing. Spending time with his family and friends brings him the most joy. Any comments concerning this book, please contact Jim by e-mail at onthedoorsteps@yahoo.com.

Printed in the United States
68310LVS00001BA/233

9 781425 982874